ADVENTURE TIME™

SUGARY SHORTS
VOLUME 3

ADVENTURE TIME: SUGARY SHORTS Volume Three, September 2017. Published by KaBOOM!, a division of Boom Entertainment, Inc.

BOOM! Studios, 5670 Wilshire Boulevard, Suite 450, Los Angeles, CA 90036-5679. Printed in China. First Printing.

ISBN: 978-1-68415-030-4, eISBN: 978-1-61398-707-0

ADVENTURE TIME™
CREATED BY
PENDLETON WARD

"SNOW HOPE"
Written and Illustrated by
LUKE PEARSON

"PUPS IN PERIL"
Written and Illustrated by
JEREMY SORESE

"A SOUR WINTER"
Written and Illustrated by
T. ZYSK

""EYE SCREAM"
Written by
JANET ROSE & ALLISON STREJLAU
Illustrated by
ALLISON STREJLAU

"ONCE UPON A TIME"
Written by
FRANK GIBSON
Illustrated by
BECKY DREISTADT
Lettered by Britt Wilson

"SHORT CAKES"
Written and Illustrated by
IAN MCGINTY
Colored and Lettered by Fred C. Stresing

"AMBITREACHEROUS!"
Written and Illustrated by
ANDY HIRSCH

Cover by
VICTORIA MADERNA

"GROCERY TIME!"
Written by
ZACK SMITH
Illustrated by
BRAD MCGINTY

"BEACH BUM BOOGIE"
Written and Illustrated by
ZACK GIALLONGO

"BOOTY AND THE BEAST"
Written by
JEN BENNETT
Illustrated by
EMILY WARREN
Lettered by Hannah Nance Partlow

"A BUN'S LIFE"
Written and Illustrated by
KRISTEN NESS

"SPHAGNUM SHMAGNUM"
Written and Illustrated by
JAMES THE STANTON

"JELLY WARS"
Written by
ERIC M. ESQUIVEL
Illustrated by
PHIL JACOBSON

Designer
KARA LEOPARD

Associate Editor
ALEX GALER

Editor
WHITNEY LEOPARD

With Special Thanks to Marisa Marionakis, Janet No, Curtis Lelash, Conrad Montgomery, Meghan Bradley, Kelly Crews, Scott Malchus, Adam Muto and the wonderful folks at Cartoon Network.

SNOW HOPE

ISSUE TWENTY SIX COVER A
HANNAH BISCHAK

"SNOW HOPE" BY LUKE PEARSON
HEY CHECK OUT THESE SWEET NEW WOOLLY JUMPERS I JUST BOUGHT.
SIGH... THEY LOOK SNUGGLY AS ALL HECK.
IF ONLY IT WOULD SNOW ALREADY. I FEEL LIKE I'VE BEEN WAITING FOR EVER.
IT'S SNOWING
JAKE, QUICK, GET IN BED!
YOUR BED.
THE SOONER WE FALL ASLEEP, THE SOONER WE CAN-

-WAKE UP!

AND GO PLAY IN THAT SWEET, SWEET SNOW.

OH MAN, I AM SO READY FOR...

THIS?

NO SNOW, HUH?
I CAN'T UNDERSTAND IT...

IT...IT MUST HAVE...

BEEN STOLEN.

I DON'T KNOW MAN, IT PROBABLY JUST ME
THINK ABOUT IT.

WHO DO WE KNOW THAT'S INTO SNOW IN A BIG WAY?

"AT ONCE A VOICE AROSE AMONG THE BLEAK TWIGS OVERHEAD."
HEY! HEY, ICE KING! YOU CROOK!
"...IN A FULL-HEARTED EVENSONG, OF JOY ILLIMITED."
GUNTER
KEEP OUT
I DON'T KNOW IF 'ILLIMITED' IS A REAL WORD GUNTER, BUT THESE POEMS ARE REALLY VERY GOOD.
WAAK
GIVE US BACK OUR SNOW.
WHAT SNOW? MY SNOW?
OUR SNOW.
YOU DON'T HAVE ANY SNOW!
BECAUSE YOU TOOK IT!
IT'S ALWAYS THERE!
LIAR!

HA
HA
HEH

WHOOP.
HA HA
HOOO

ALRIGHT, WHAT'S THE DEAL, WHY ARE YOU LAUGHING AND FOOLING AROUND..?

IN YOUR MAD, UNJUSTIFIED RAGE, ICE KING, YOU'VE GIVEN US EXACTLY THAT WHICH WE SOUGHT.

I CLAIM THAT AS A VICTORY FOR SUPERIOR MINDS.

IF YOU WANTED TO JUST ROLL AROUND IN THE SNOW LIKE A COUPLE OF BABIES, YOU COULD JUST COME TO THE ICE KINGDOM.

YOU KNOW, WHERE IT'S ALWAYS SNOWING?

NO MAN, YOU DON'T GET IT.

IT'S NOT THAT MUCH FUN WHEN IT'S ALWAYS THERE. WE LIKE THAT IT'S ON TOP OF THE NORMAL STUFF.

HM.. OW... OUCH
YOU OKAY, BUDDY?

THIS JUMPER... IT'S GOTTEN ALL SUPER ITCHY AND TIGHT SUDDENLY.

DRY SKIN. JOIN THE FLAKE CLUB. GOT SOME CREAM IF YOU WANT IN.
MY HEAD... IT FEELS...

..ALL WOOLLY.
UM... FINN?

I AM NOT FINN. I AM THE CHILLBEATER! THE SNUGBRINGER.

KNITTED IN THE DEPTHS FROM THE WOOL OF THE GREAT GOAT OF THE BELOW.

ALWAYS, I SERVE HIM TIRELESSLY, ENDLESSLY STRIVING—

—TO CAPTURE AND SUBDUE ALL THINGS COLD AND NON-COSY.

IT IS HIS WISH. IT IS HIS BIDDING.
CAPTURE AND SUBDUE! CAPTURE AND SUBDUE!

WHERE DID YOU SAY YOU GOT THESE JUMPERS FROM AGAIN?

JUST FROM THIS RANDOM DUDE I MET.

HE SEEMED LEGIT TO ME.

WE SHOULD PROBABLY GO STOP THAT THING FROM EATING THE ICE KINGDOM, RIGHT?
RIGHT.

SPEAKING OF... WHERE IS ICE KING?
HE MUST HAVE BABIED OUT.

HEY FINN, DO YOU RECKON MY JUMPER'S OK OR SHOULD I TAKE IT OFF, JUST IN CASE?

EHH, IT'S PROBABLY FINE. COME ON.

END.

PUPS IN PERIL

ISSUE TWENTY EIGHT, COVER B

KYLA VANDERKLUGT

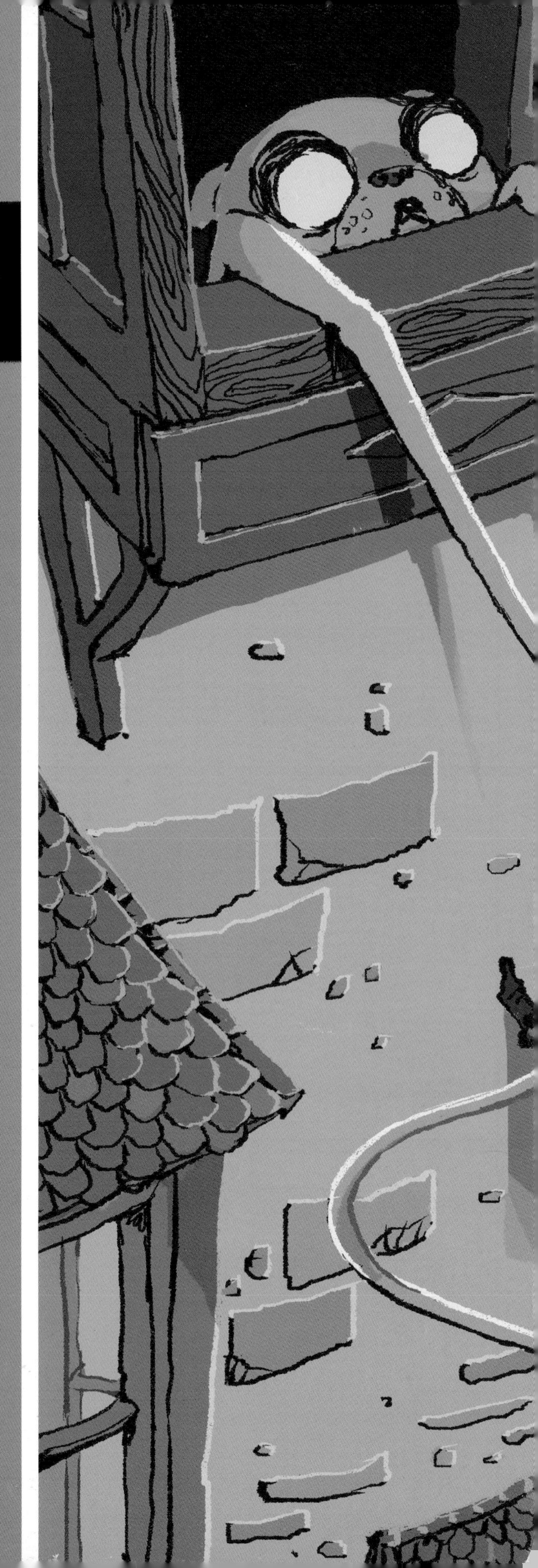

BUT I'M NOT A HOT DOG! HONEST!
ALL DOGS ARE A DANGER TO THE KINGDOM.
AND UNTIL THAT HORRIBLE HOT DOG HAS BEEN CAPTURED HERE YOU WILL WAIT.
BUT... HOT... DOG... WHAT?
BMO! TREE TRUNKS!
GO FIND THE FIRE PUP!
GREEN DOG, COME BACK HERE!
¡HUFF!
OKEE DOKE.
PUPS in PERIL
by: Jeremy Sorese for Jon Chad

AHHHHH
AHHH
BOO!
QUICK QUICK
OH NO
SPLASH
OH NO INDEED
DO YOU EVEN KNOW WHAT A HOT DOG IS, KING DUDE?

DRIP
HURRY!
HURRY!
HURRY!
HURRY!
ONWARD, BRAVE STALLION.
DRIP
DRIP
DRIP
BMO, I'M NOT A SCALLION.
PADDLE PADDLE
YES IT IS A YOU.
YOU ARE A HOT DOG. SEE, LOOK AT YOU SWEAT.
NO, NO, NO I AM A JAKE AND I GLOW, I DO NOT SWEAT.

DRIP
WOW LOOK.
THEY ARE TRYING TO REFREEZE THE CITY.
1 2 AND A 3! LET IT SNOW!
WHOOSH
DRIP
DRIP
AR-O-O-O-O-O
HEH HEH HEH
BUT I CAN SEE YOU IN A LITTLE BUN...
LIKE THIS...
NO

OLLY OLLY OXEN FREE, FIRE PUP!
GASP
FIRE PUP!!!
DRIP
AROOO
AROOOO
I AM A JAKE!
YOU NON-COOL CAT KING! DEAL WITH IT!

STOP! HALT! WAIT! PLEASE!
BRACE FOR IMPACT!
oOf
DRIP
DRIP
DRIP
DRIP
WEEEEEEEEE
!
ARF

DRIP
DRIP
STOP RIGHT THERE!
NO ESCAPE NOW, LITTLE GREEN DOG AND TELEVISION.
DRIP
DRIP
DRIP
DRIP
DRIP

GURGLE GURGLE

PEW!

HA
USELESS.
OH NO WE ARE TRAPPED.
PANT PANT

FIRE PUP. RELAX!

THUNK

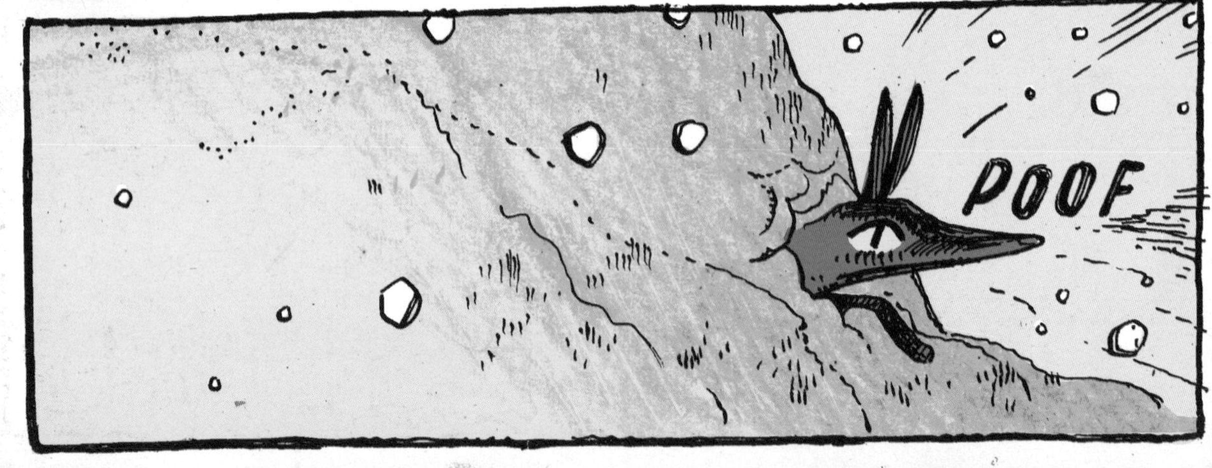
POOF

WOOF
WOOF
WOOF
YA!

BARK

BUT... NO, WAIT, YOU'RE OUR PRISONER.

YAY
ARF!
THE END

A SOUR WINTER

ISSUE TWENTY EIGHT COVER C
JAMES LLOYD

"A Sour Winter"
by T. Zysk
hn?
hhhnnnnnnnnnnnn
hee hee
ha ha
Repulsive.
Splut
SO DISTURBING!

The winter is a liar. Look at it.
This "snow", it falls and sits on the ground like a lovely blanket...
But IN REALITY it's just cold, devious rain that gets your pants and boots all damp.
And not the NICE kind of damp.
I will have to write the Princess a letter of complaint...
But no, it would take too long with this. NGH. WEATHER.
She must hear my grievances immediately and loudly to fully understand how important they are.
But I need a way to reach the Candy Kingdom without being exposed.
DUNGEON
No.
NO.
I will not stand for any wetting of pants on this day!

shf
shf
KLANG
KLANG
PZZZZ
ZZZZ
kene
fwpwp
YES.
I will save us all from these vulgar atmospheric conditions.
I will SAVE THE EARLDOM.
Earldom of Lemongrab Resident 2 of 2
LEMON IS NO
Oho.
Oho.
You see I have invented this fantastic snow-resistant suit.
I am truly talented and underappreciated.
Hnngh, look at this DIRE INSULT. Your wretched loveliness doesn't fool me.
Sometimes it doesn't bother me that no one is listening to me.

Sometimes it is less lonely than other times.
It's... learning to imitate.
ENEMY.
ENEMY.
stmp
stmp
W-hat-
Can't... MOVE...
W-ha-!
ENEMY
H-how?
You don't even have a hard dr-
shoopp

MUST DESTROY WINTER.
LEMONSUIT WILL DESTROY WINTER.
Z Z Z
ZKKKNNK-
SShhsss s shh
shshhh
VENTING TRANSMISSION FLUID AND FUEL.
PLEASE WAIT.
SYSTEM SHUT DOWN.
DEATH WITH HONOR.
foomph
U-un...
accept...

CONGRAT LEMONGUY

Not the war.
NEVER THE WAR.
YOU WILL REGRET THIS NIGHT.

WEEKS LATER.

Princess, I have done
what I can to combat t
foul enemy, but now tha
I have fallen ill, you mu
not stand idly by and
allow this to continue.
I urge you to mobilize
quickly and impose a v
harshly enforced ban o
winter in the Earldom o
mongrab, if not the
ole of the Candy
Kingdom.
This includes, but is
not limited to, snow,
snowplay, snowcrafts
folk songs about sno
water that is below
room temperature, ho
days that take place
winter, rain that falls
too slowly, books ab

Written Complai
Earl of Lemongrab's Written Complaints

I really wish he'd find a hobby.
I thought getting angry WAS his hobby. He's really great at it.
END

EYE SCREAM

ADVENTURE TIME WINTER SPECIAL 2014 COVER B
T. ZYSK

EYE SCREAM

Written by Janet Rose and Allison Strejlau
Illustration by Allison Strejlau

OH YEAH, ICE PICNICS ARE THE BEST!
HAND ME OVER THAT SYRUPY GOODNESS, MY MAN!

HOW DO THEY EXPECT ME TO WARM MY DELICIOUS APPLE PIES WITH A LITTLE FLAME LIKE THAT?

OH WHOOPSIES!
TREE TRUNKS, NO!!!

THE CEILING'S GIVING IN!
CREAK
GUYS, I THINK WE GOTTA MOVE IT!
I GOT THIS!
WHAT'S THAT NOISE?!
AOOOEEEE
OEEEEEEE
OOO
SNAP
GROAN
C'MON!
I DON'T GOT THIS!!

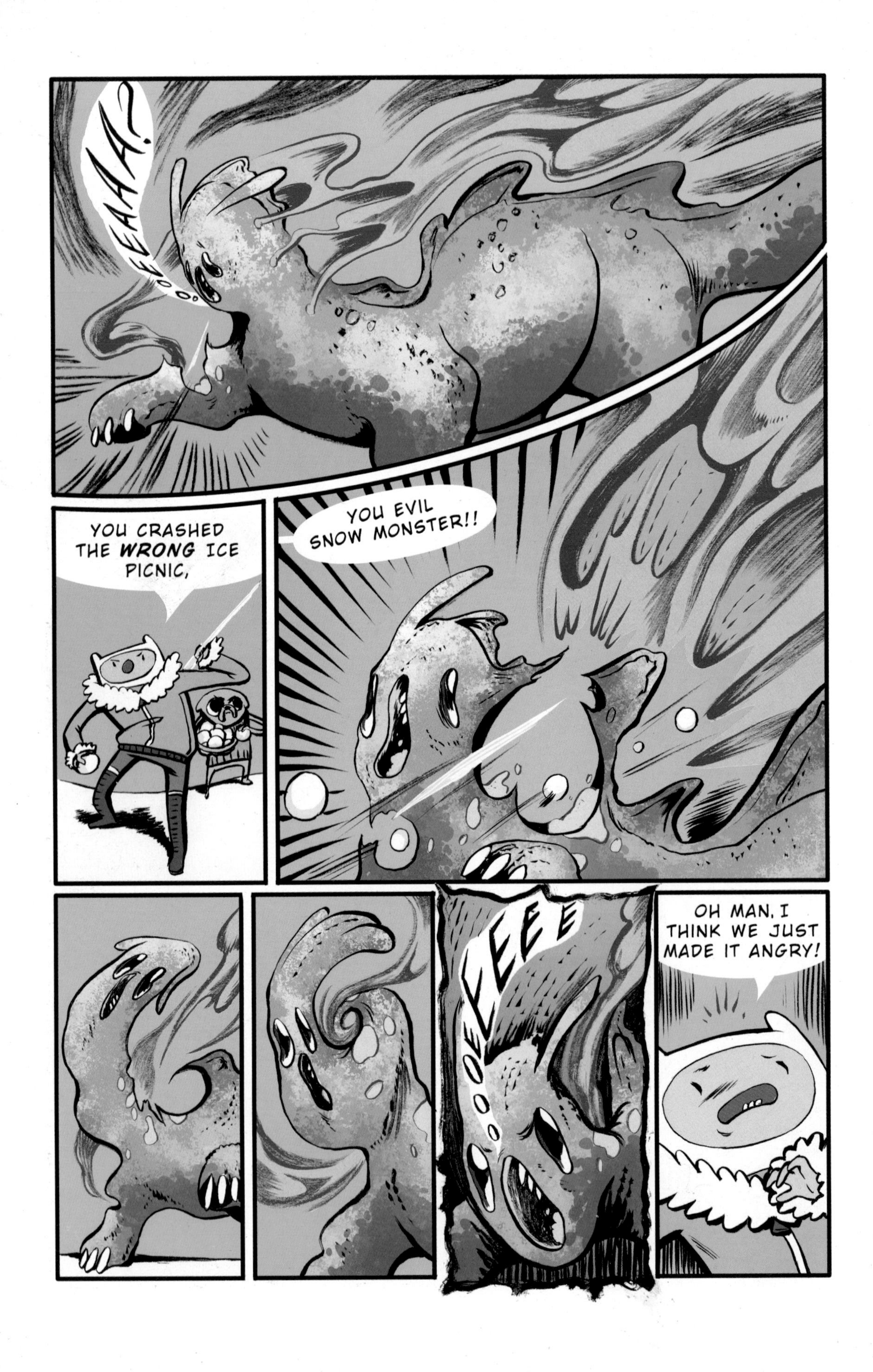
EEEAAA?
YOU CRASHED THE WRONG ICE PICNIC,
YOU EVIL SNOW MONSTER!!
OEEEEE
OH MAN, I THINK WE JUST MADE IT ANGRY!

IT WON'T MATTER WHEN THEY'RE IN HALF!

MAYBE IF WE KEEP AT IT HE WON'T BE ABLE TO REFORM!
YEAAAAA

AH!

STOP!!

STOP ATTACKING HIM YOU GUYS, THEY DIDN'T MEAN IT!

WHAT DO YOU MEAN, TREE TRUNKS?
?

YEAH, THIS GUY IS TRYING TO RUIN OUR ICE PICNIC, DUDE!

HE ISN'T A "SNOW" CREATURE, HE'S A "FRIED ICE CREAM" CREATURE!!

WHAT?

I MADE HIM BY ACCIDENT WHILE I WAS WORKING ON SOME NEW PIE RECIPIES!

HE JUST GOT TOO EXCITED WHEN I SAID HE COULD COME ALONG!

I'M SORRY I SURPRISED YOU LADS, BUT MY LADY MAKER SAID YOU MAY BE IN NEED OF SOME WARMTH AND I WISHED TO OFFER MY SERVICES BUT I MAY HAVE PANICKED WHEN I HEARD MISS TRUNKS YELP IN SURPRISE.

SEE? I'M ALL GOOEY AND WARM ON THE INSIDE! I'M SORRY I GOT EXCITED, I JUST REALLY WANTED TO MEET YOU GUYS AFTER EVERYTHING I'VE HEARD!

MAN I'M SORRY FRIED ICE CREAM CREATURE, WE WERE JERKS!
YEAH MAYBE WE SHOULDN'T ALWAYS COME TO A CONCLUSION OF DOOM WHENEVER WE MEET SOMEONE NEW.
UNLESS THEY'RE STRAWBERRY FLAVORED!

HA
HA
HA
HA
MARCY NO!!
The End

ONCE UPON A TIME

ISSUE TWENTY SEVEN COVER A
BRITTNEY WILLIAMS

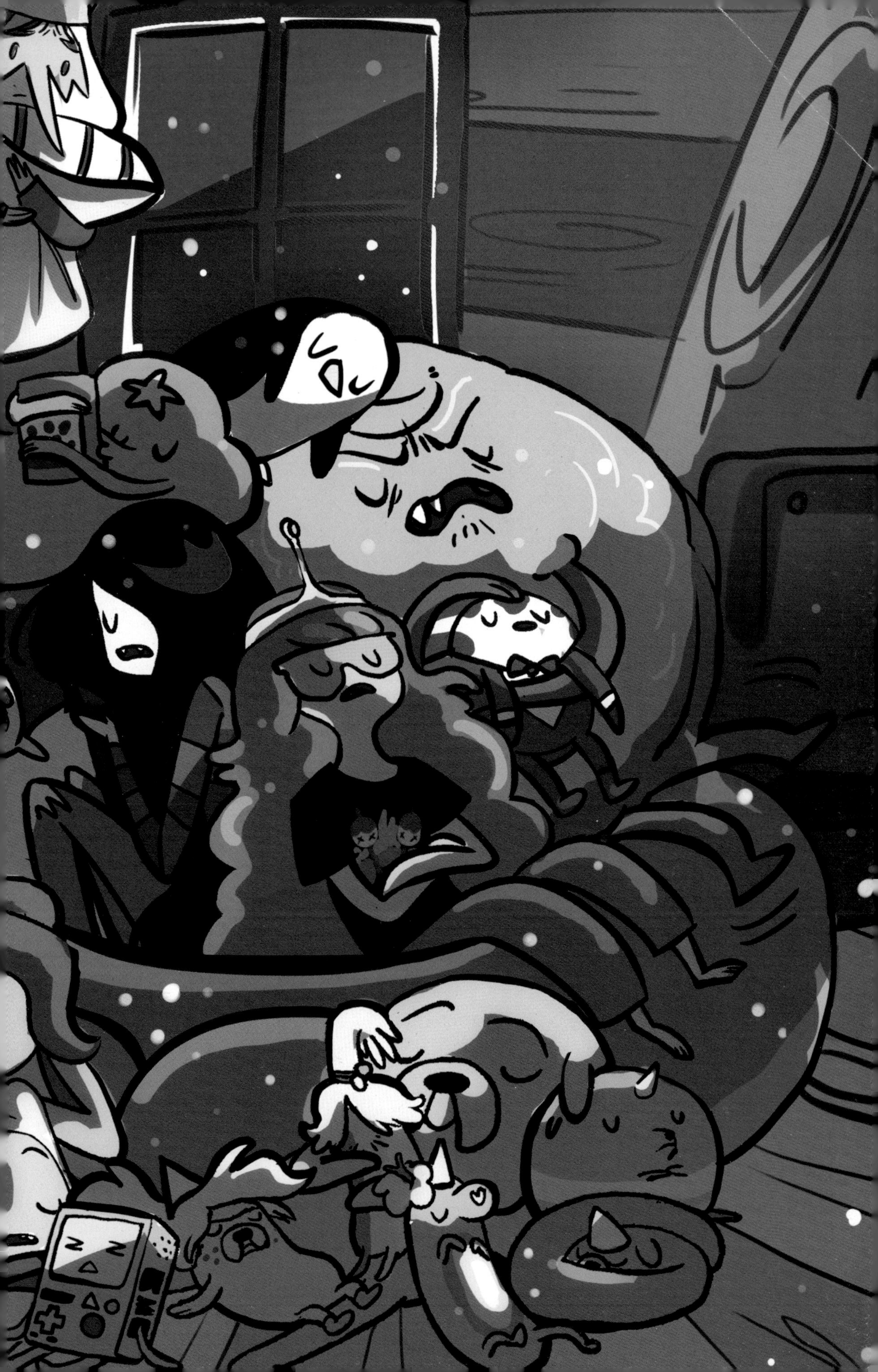

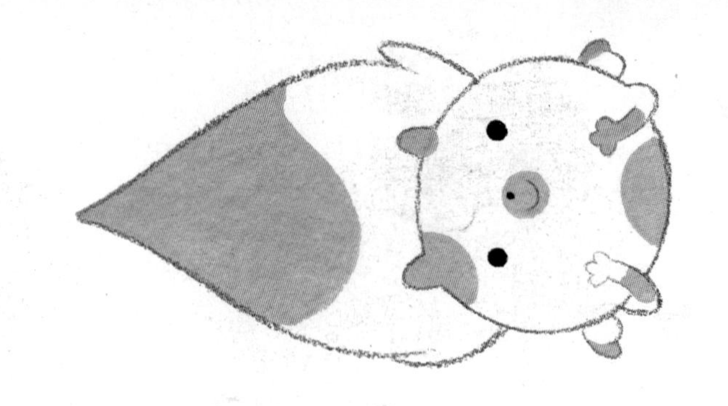

Once upon a time, there was a little hero.
She was the bravest, best behaved little hero the land of OOO had ever seen.
She reduced the scariest monsters to the tiniest inconveniences.
She studied hard,
helped her parents,
and best little hero anyone could ask for.
IDEAS

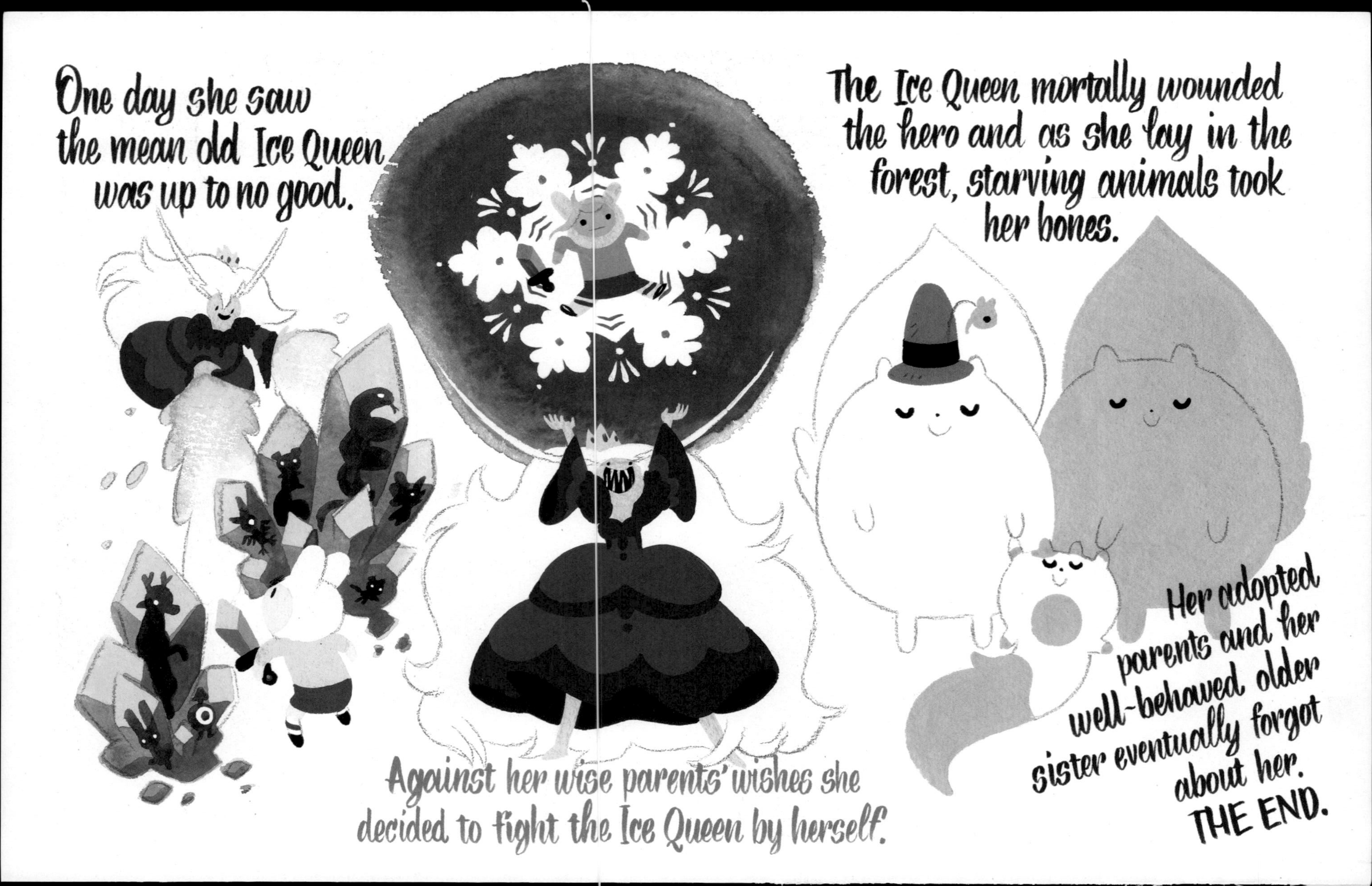
One day she saw the mean old Ice Queen was up to no good.
Against her wise parents' wishes she decided to fight the Ice Queen by herself.
The Ice Queen mortally wounded the hero and as she lay in the forest, starving animals took her bones.
Her adopted parents and her well-behaved older sister eventually forgot about her.
THE END.

That is SO BOGUS!

SHUT.

. . .

Pretty cool story, right?

What's the moral of *that* supposed to be?
It doesn't matter if you do the right thing if you are told not to do it?
that would be doing the WRONG thing!
No, that would be doing NO-thing.
Get it?
Ugh. All I wanted for my birthday was a cool dangerous adventure in the night.
No, you also wanted a big old birthday cake and a party.
Haha, yeah.
Did you send out the invitations?
I certainly did!
RSVP
PRINCE GUMBALL
CAKE

With that taken care of, I'm going to bed!

And by that I mean, sneaking out and playing in the forest!

I don't know about this, Fionna!

OOOF!

How come we can play out here during the day and not at night?
It's not like anything changes.
I guess you have a point...

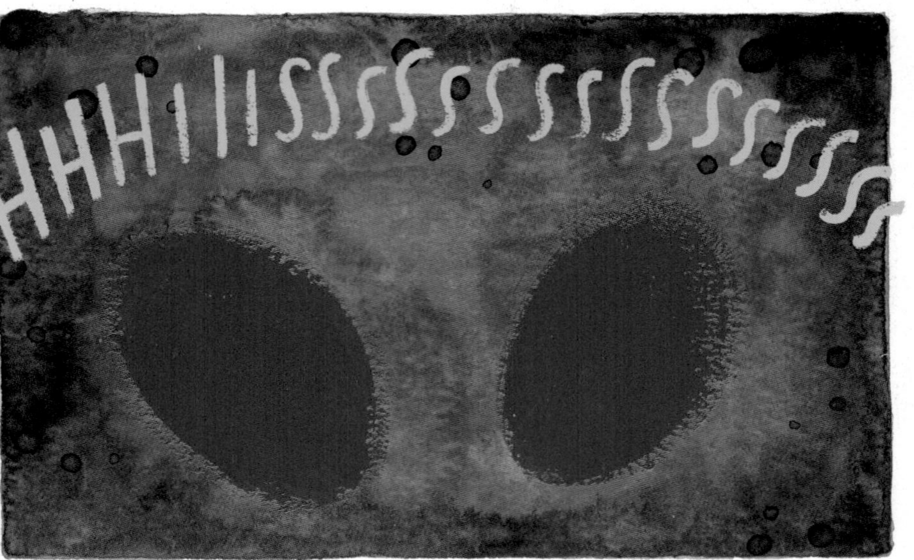

See?
HHHISSSSSSS
Hey man, don't be like that.
Sorry, I thought you were a monster or something!
It's just night!
There's nothing to be afraid of!
If there are no monsters during the day, there won't be any at night!
You haven't told her?

You didn't tell her?
We've been kinda building up to it.

What the heck is that?

Is that Prince Gumball?!
That's the Ice Queen.

That's nothing, pumpkin! We should probably get back inside. Goodbye, Mr. Squirrel.
I'm outta here!
The Ice Queen is REAL?!
We were waiting for the right time to tell you!
THAT'S SO AWESOME!

I'm gonna go kick her butt now.
NO NO NO NO!!
Mom is going to throw a fit!

I'd better find a sword.
Please, Fionna! I'm meant to stop you from getting into trouble!

Wait, where'd you find a sword?

Over there!

I JUST THINK THIS WORKS BETTER!
I just don't understand!
You could just visit the castle and make an appointment like everyone else...

You can just come hang out whenever you want!
BUT WHAT IF I WANT TO HANG OUT ALL THE TIME?

You really aren't taking my feelings into account here.

NO, NOT THIS TIME! EVERY TIME YOU TRICK ME AND ESCAPE SOMEHOW! YOU CRAWL OUT A WINDOW, MAYBE YOU'LL SUMMON YOUR ARMY TO RETRIEVE YOU! BUT THIS TIME YOU WON'T EVEN WANT TO LEAVE.
I'm pretty sure I already want to leave...

WHAT DOES LITTLE GUMBALL LOVE MORE THAN BEING SURROUNDED BY HIS CANDY FRIENDS?
NOTHING!

NOW YOU'LL BE SURROUNDED BY CANDY... FOREVER.

But someone else will just rescue him! They always do!
Don't be a scaredy cake!
UNCOOL FIONNA!

We've lived next to the Ice Queen this entire time?

FIONNA!
PUFF
PUFF
I'm f-fine!

Girl, you don't look fine.

I'm totally fine.
I landed safely in this pile of totally non-scary penguins.

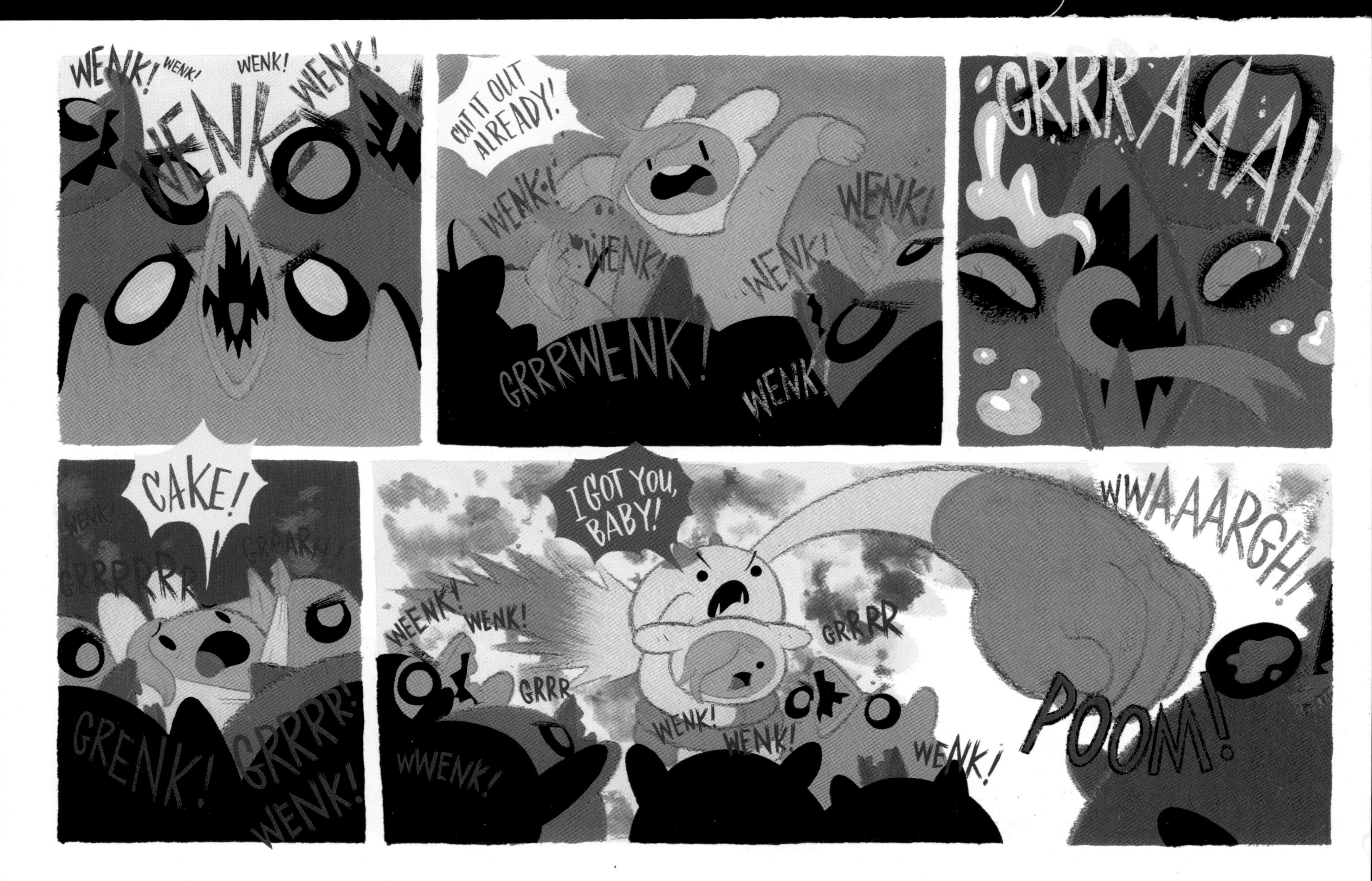

WENK! WENK! WENK! WENK!
WENK!
CUT IT OUT ALREADY!
WENK!
WENK!
WENK!
WENK!
GRRRWENK!
WENK!
¡GRRRAAAH!
CAKE!
WENK!
GRRRRRR
GRRARR!
GRENK!
GRRRR!
WENK!
I GOT YOU, BABY!
WEENK!
WENK!
GRRR
GRRRR
WWENK!
WENK!
WENK!
WENK!
WWAAARGH!
POOM!

PUNT!
AIN'T NO DANG PENGUINS...
SQUISH.
...BEATING UP ON MY FIONNA!
WWEENNK...

C'mon, let's go home.

I just wanted to be treated as an adult! I'm turning six tomorrow and I want everyone to know I can handle myself...

...even though I can't.
NONSENSE! You knew when to ask for help, that's what an adult would do!

See that guy right over there?
that guy was a big baby cause he didn't ask for help.

BIG BABY

It doesn't matter, I'm going to be treated like I'm five forever.
Sigh
Let's go get that Prince.
THIS BIRTHDAY RULES!
If we get killed by the Ice Queen I'm gonna be real mad!

SLAM
I bet we needed that door, huh?
We're in a maze!

A delicious maze!

DON'T EAT THE ICE QUEEN'S POISON CAKE MAZE!

SMACK

FIIIIINE.

That Ice Queen really gets on my nerves.

Poison Cake! What a butt!

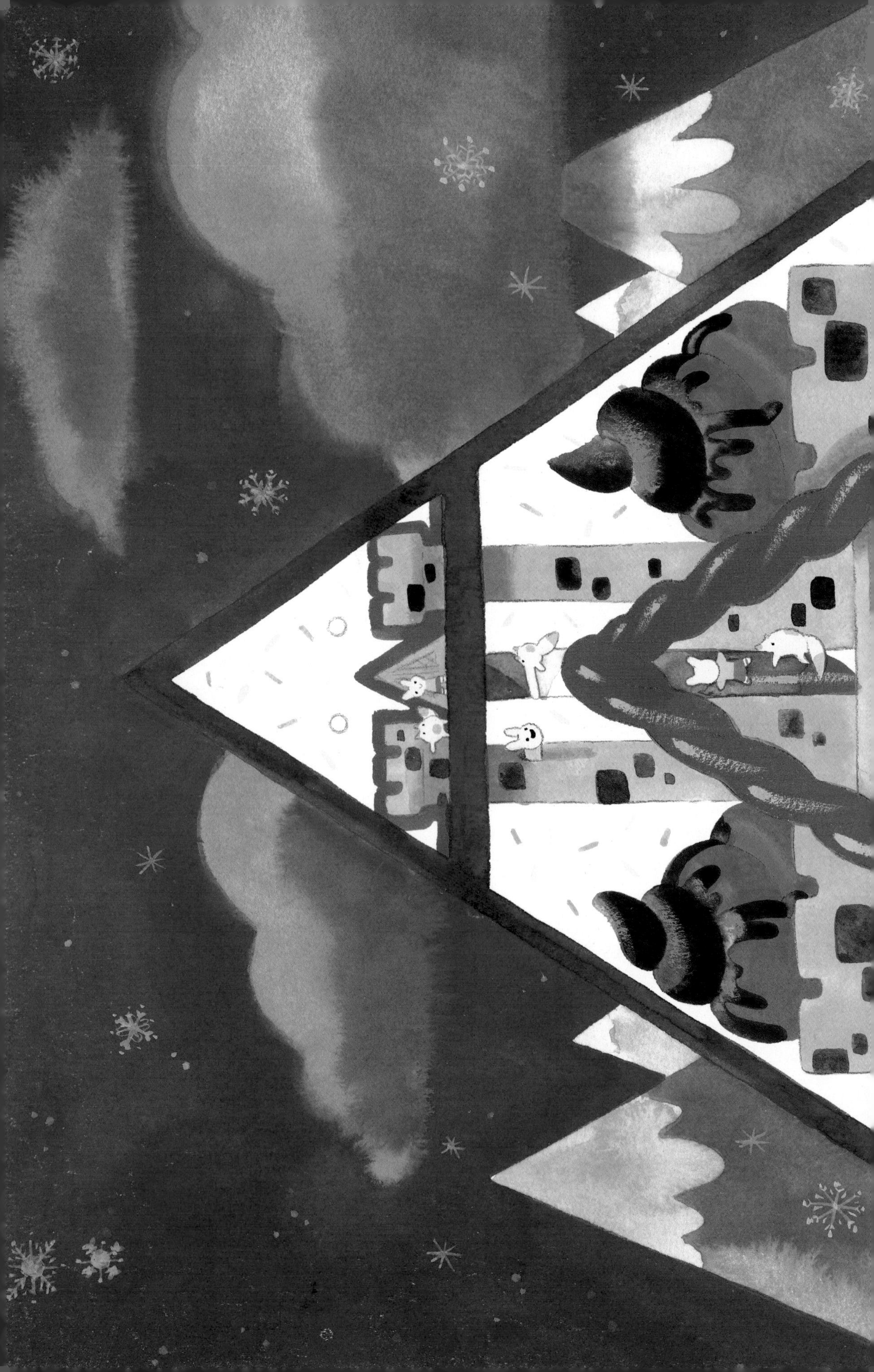

EEEK!
EEEAARGH!
Humph.
HA HA!
HEE HEE!

I bet he's behind here.
Why?

His name is totally on it!

He he he, it's a gumball, get it?

NNGGHHHH

Rescuing is harder than it looks.

OR IS IT?

Hey, man.

FIONNA!

I was worried I was going to miss your birthday!

CLEARLY MY COMMITMENT TO THIS BIRTHDAY CAKE THEME WAS FLAWED!

HAHAHA!
SWING
AAH!

OK YOU CAN LEAVE IF YOU DON'T BURN ME.

MONOCHROMICORN!

Thanks again for saving me. That was really cool.
Don't mention it!

I always worry that I'm such a burden, getting kidnapped all the time and wasting my kingdom's resources.

Thanks! I can't wait for your party tomorrow!
You'll be MY burden now, I mean, uh, I like rescuing people!

YOU BETTER BE ON TIME!

Oh glob, no, one is coming.
Don't worry, honey! They probably just hit traffic!
TICK

TICK

TOCK

I brought friends!
And CAKE!
That is the Coolest cake ever!
It was my idea! I wanted the cake to look like you because you're my best friend!
Also I totally wanted to devour your likeness to gain your cool stretchy powers!
HA HA HA, just kidding, but it's cool how you can stretch and stuff.
HEE HA HA HEE HA HOO HAW HA HA HA HA HA HOO HA HA HA HA HA HA
THE END!

SHORT CAKES

ISSUE TWENTY SEVEN COVER C
TOM HUNTER

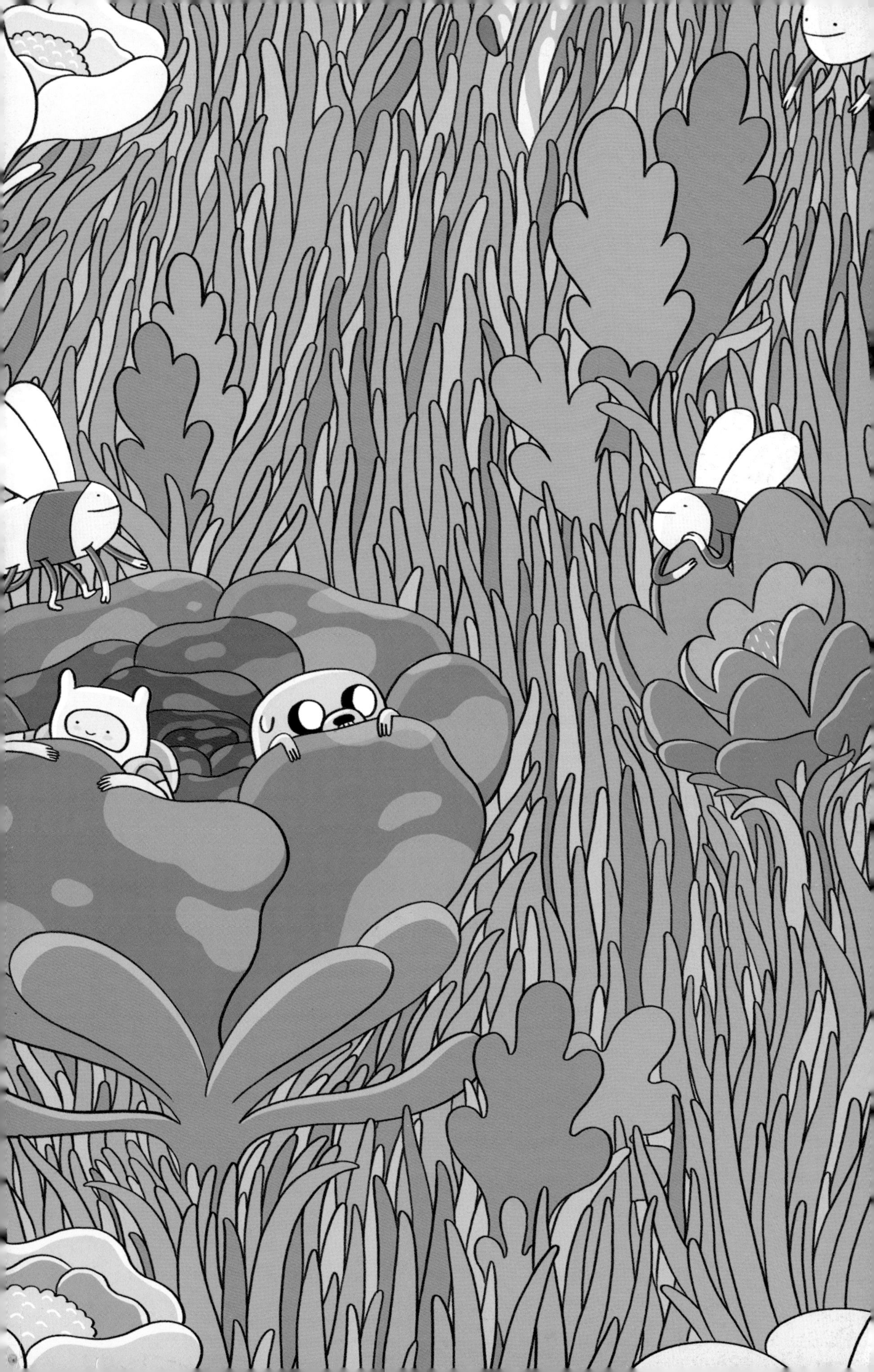

BAKE A CAKE
Cake! Where are you? Are you gonna help me show Prince Gumball how to make cupcakes, or not?
You better not be eating those things without us! I haven't even frosted 'em yet!
Where is that sneaky kitty?
Hey, Fionna, wait-
Uh-oh.
See, look, Gumbo! Baking is fun and cool! Also, you get to eat stuff! Stuff, dude!
Holy heck, Fionna, hope I can be a great baker someday! Y'know, and a prince.
Mmm!
POP
Ew! There's cat hair in the CUPCAKES!
Bleh.
I was just testing 'em, I swear!

STRANGE GUISE
Cake, I wanna stay out and keep adventurin'! It's not even dark out!
It's dark enough! 'Sides, I got my eye on some of those leftover tarts from yesterday!
And I'm gonna eat all of 'em!
They were all covered in cat hair anyway, you can have them.
I love spending time with you, Fionna.
Hey, who're those strange guys?
Beats me.
They look... kinda familiar, though.
HEY! HEYYY!!
HI. HELLO.
MM. HOWDY.
Well, that one seems nice enough.
Well, hey, you! I'm Fionna and this is Cake and BMO! What're ya'll doin' out here in the woods?!
HEY! I'm-
Can it, bud.
You never saw us here. Just look at the nice smiley face and forget...
...forget...
...forget...
...forget.
Uh, your friend is just kinda crawlin' away, dude. Is she okay?!
MAYBE. SORRY WE COULDN'T PLAY WITH YOU. UH, WE GOTTA GO, I GUESS.
...forget...
Okay, I'm definitely ready to go home now.

Let's have a SNOWBALL FIGHT!!!
SPLORT
Why is there *pee-pee* in the *snowball*??!!
Nah, it's just Lady Lemongrab playin' in the snow.
Oh.
This is *acceptable!*

THE TACO SONG
Marshall Lee! Let's start a band! A really neat rad band!
A band! Ha! That's kinda goofy, feel me?
Besides, can you even sing, Fionna?
YESSSSSSSS
Hey, dude, I love tacos.
Oh, I've already got a song about tacos.
Oh, those tacos in your eyes,
They make me wanna cry...
Estes pastéis nos teus olhos,
Eles paracern ser tão gostosos!*
Those tacos in your eyes...
*That's Portuguese!

LUMPSTACHE
Oh, hey, Lumpy Space Prince! Why're you rubbin' your face like that, dude? Got a booger?
Heh. Booger.
RUB
RUB
RUB
RUB
OH. MY. GLOB. Not that it's any of your business but I'm trying to grow a sweet mustache!
I want, like, the bushiest, most manliest 'stache ever... and I'm gonna keep rubbin' until-
HOLD UP.
Are you tellin' me if we rub our faces we could grow gnarly mustaches?! Is that what you're sayin'?!
Pshh. Uh, yeah, dude, like everyone knows that.
RUB
RUB
RUB
RUB
RUB
RUB
RUB
IAN MCGINTY 2014

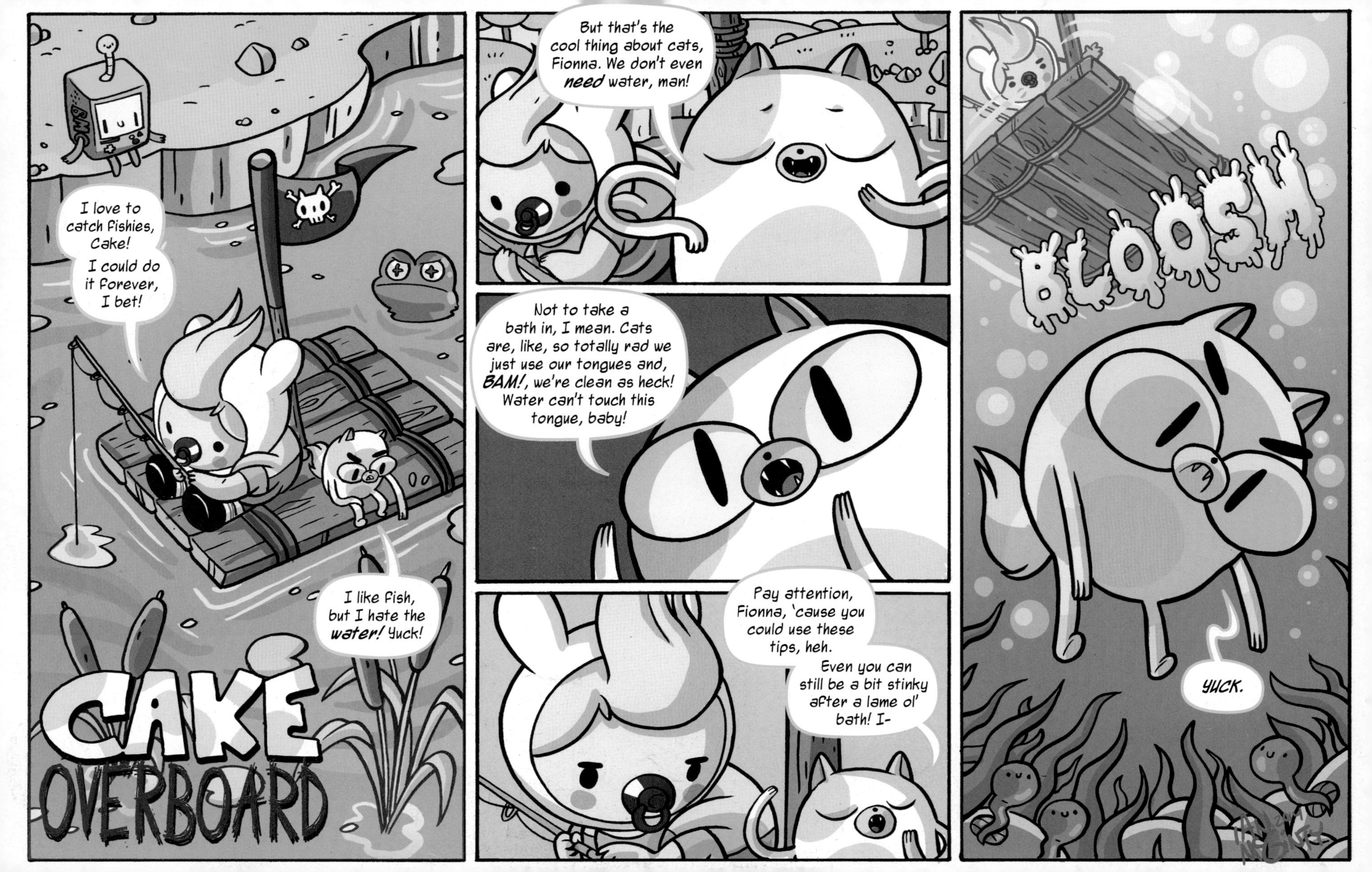
CAKE OVERBOARD
I love to catch fishies, Cake!
I could do it forever, I bet!
I like fish, but I hate the *water!* Yuck!
But that's the cool thing about cats, Fionna. We don't even ***need*** water, man!
Not to take a bath in, I mean. Cats are, like, so totally rad we just use our tongues and, ***BAM!***, we're clean as heck! Water can't touch this tongue, baby!
Pay attention, Fionna, 'cause you could use these tips, heh.
Even you can still be a bit stinky after a lame ol' bath! I-
BLOOSH
YUCK.

AMBITREACHEROUS!

ISSUE TWENTY SEVEN COVER D
CHRYSTIN GARLAND

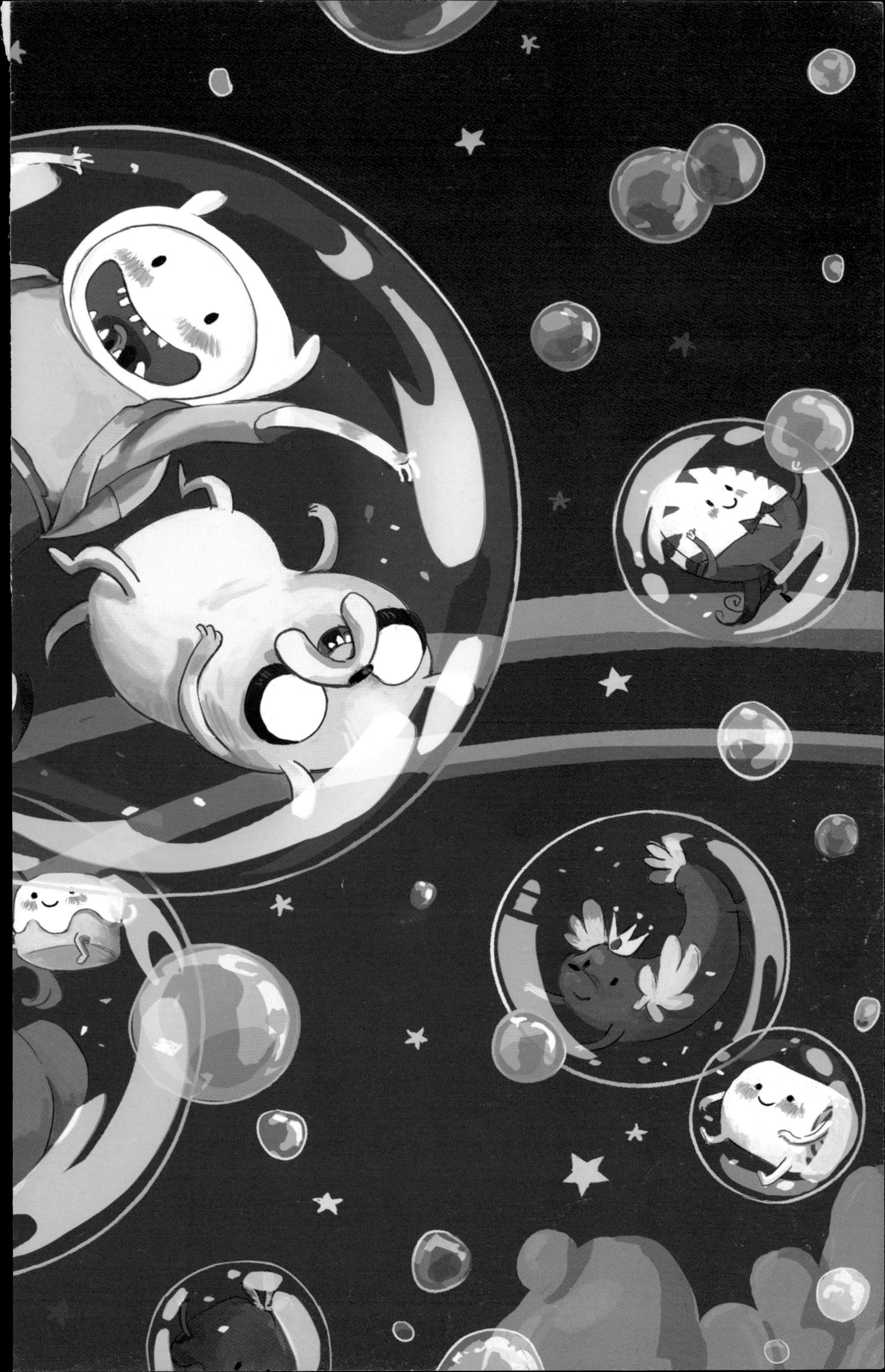

AMBITREACHEROUS
by ANDY HIRSCH
ME FIRST! FLIP THIS BABY OVER TO THE BACK! I'M HAVIN' A PICNIC!
Psst... YO, I'VE GOT YOUR PAL, FRIEND.
HUH?
...JAKE. I'VE KIDNAPPED JAKE.
BMO
WHAAAAA?!

huff
huff

COME ON!
pant
YOU IN THERE, BUDDY?

JAKE?

Oof!

WHAT THE HECKS?
THIS WAY!

BUH?!

YAH!

WHOA!

HUP!

GRR...

WHERE'S JAKE?!
shh... IT'S A SURP-

PUNCH

OW!
GIMME BACK MY BUDDY, YA BIG TOOT!

I- I DON'T HAVE HIM! IT'S MY BROTHER'S BIRTHDAY, AND I WANTED YOU TO BE A SURPRISE GUEST!
I'M SO SORRY I TRICKED YOU, BUT YOU NEVER ANSWERED MY INVITATION!
WE HAVE A MAILBOX?
I DON'T CHECK THE MAIL!
JAKE!
AW, NO WAY! I CAN'T BELIEVE YOU GOT HIM!

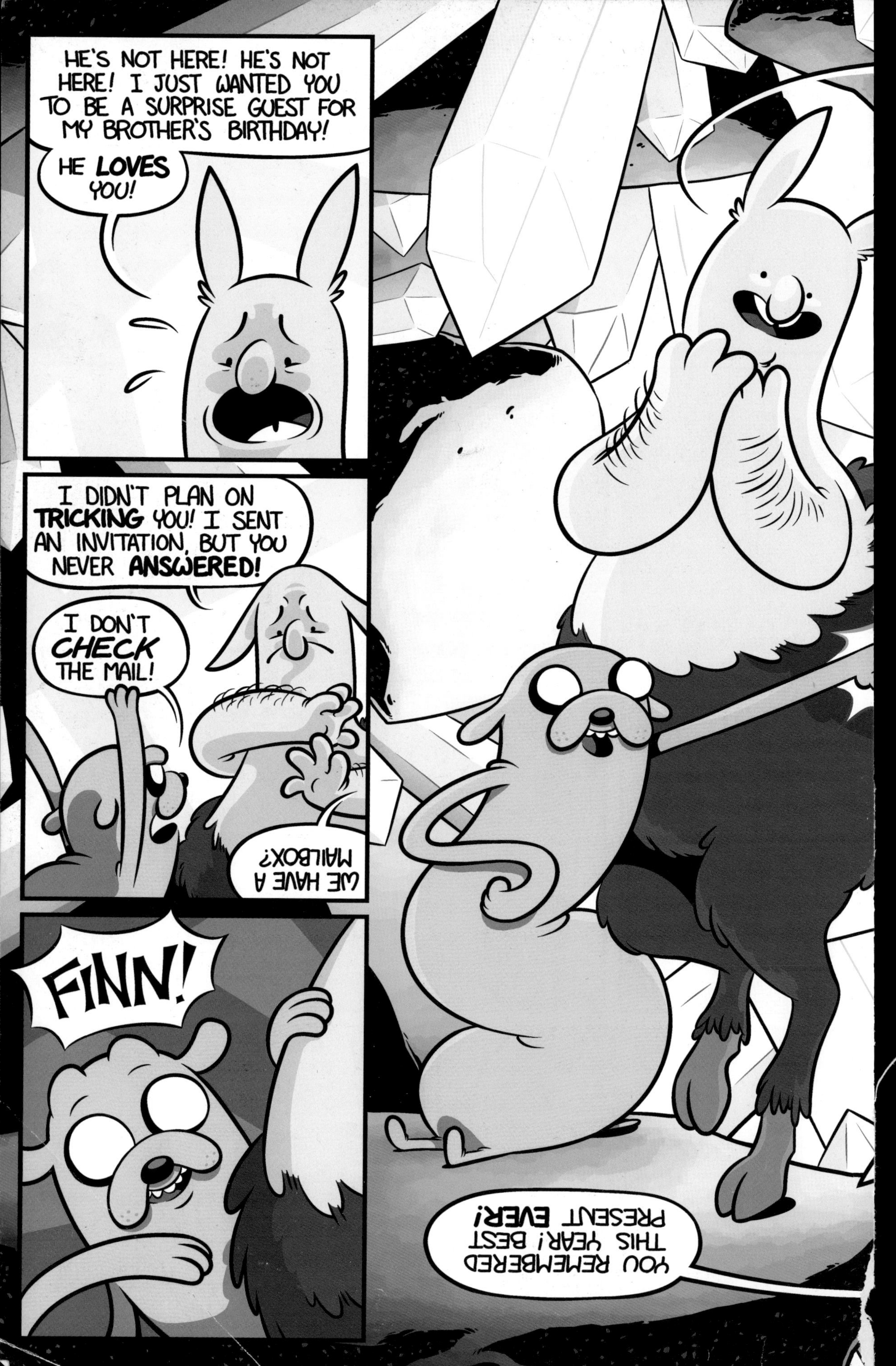
HE'S NOT HERE! HE'S NOT HERE! I JUST WANTED YOU TO BE A SURPRISE GUEST FOR MY BROTHER'S BIRTHDAY!
HE LOVES YOU!
I DIDN'T PLAN ON TRICKING YOU! I SENT AN INVITATION, BUT YOU NEVER ANSWERED!
I DON'T CHECK THE MAIL!
WE HAVE A MAILBOX?
FINN!
YOU REMEMBERED THIS YEAR! BEST PRESENT EVER!

GIMME BACK MY PAL, BOZO!
OW!

SOCK!

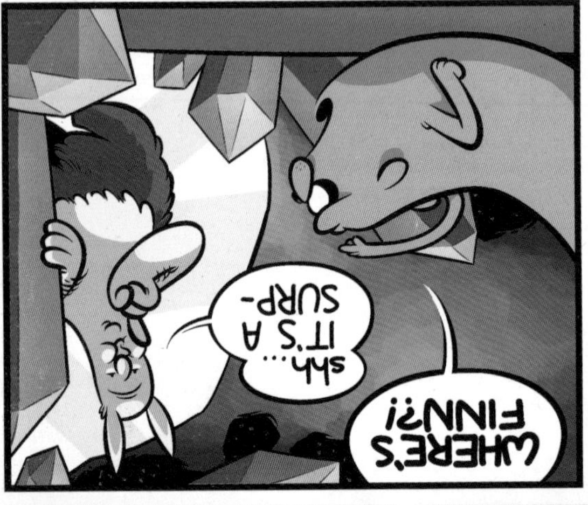
WHERE'S FINN?!
shh... IT'S A SURP-

HEY!

BUDDY?

FINN?

GUY?

OOF!

OVER HERE!
DANG.

AMBITREACHEROUS
by ANDY HIRSCH
WHY AM I UPSIDE DOWN? FLIP IT BACK!
Psst... HEY, I'VE GOT YOUR FRIEND, PAL.
HUH?
...FINN. I'VE KIDNAPPED FINN.
WHAAAAA?!

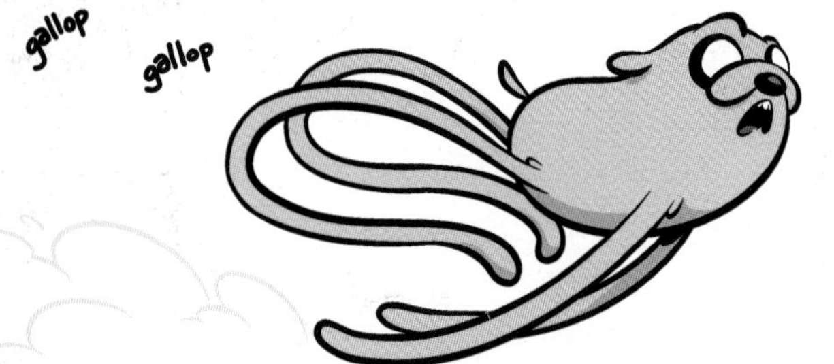
gallop
gallop

IN HERE!
AW, MAN!

FINN?

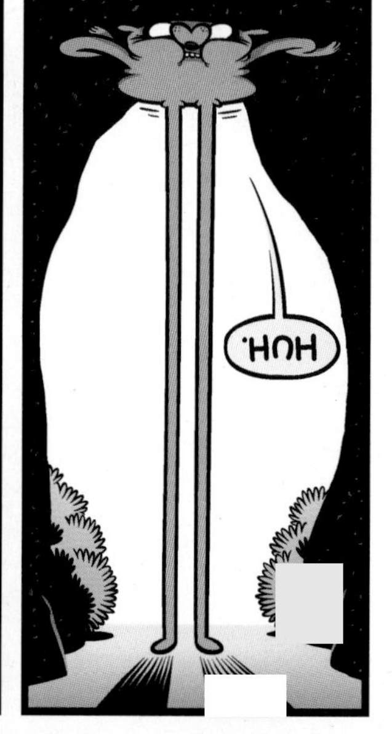
HUH.

GROCERY TIME!

ISSUE TWENTY SIX COVER D
VICKY BARKER

It was party time in the Birthday Kingdom,
The greatest ever seen!
But the awesome soiree soon was blown...
...when someone said...
Yo, we're out of ice cream!
GASP!
GAPE!
Birthday Princess declared a crisis!
It's a state of emergency!
sugar... ...buzz... fading...
They needed a hero pure and righteous!
NOTHUNG*!
"Nothung"=the sword, not "nothing." It's confusing.
A hero like...
....BILLY!

'Sup
BILLY!
IN GROCERY TIME
PART 1 Written by Zack Smith
Art by Brad McGinty
Billy had to fly or the party would die,
So off to the Grocery Kingdom he went!
REMEMBER: GET PEANUTS.
And he got a ride from his friend in the sky,
The Ancient Psychic Tandem War Elephant!
Billy usually got his food at the Squeeze-E-Mart!
The Grocery Kingdom was an unfamiliar place!
HAM CHUNK JUICE
EAT FLAKIES
KIM CHI
DRINK TOTAL SODA
SOY
HONEY
But though he was from a world apart...
This was a challenge Billy had to face!

So through the Kingdom Billy ran...
NK
...Leaving all obstacles...
IWAAAANNTITTTTT!
TOY-LETS
FLUSH AWAY HUNGER
FREE
...in his wake!
TRY OUR SAAAAMMMPLEESS!
ICE CREAM PENINSULA
But when he finally reached his goal...
Maybe later!
...he knew he'd made a terrible mistake!

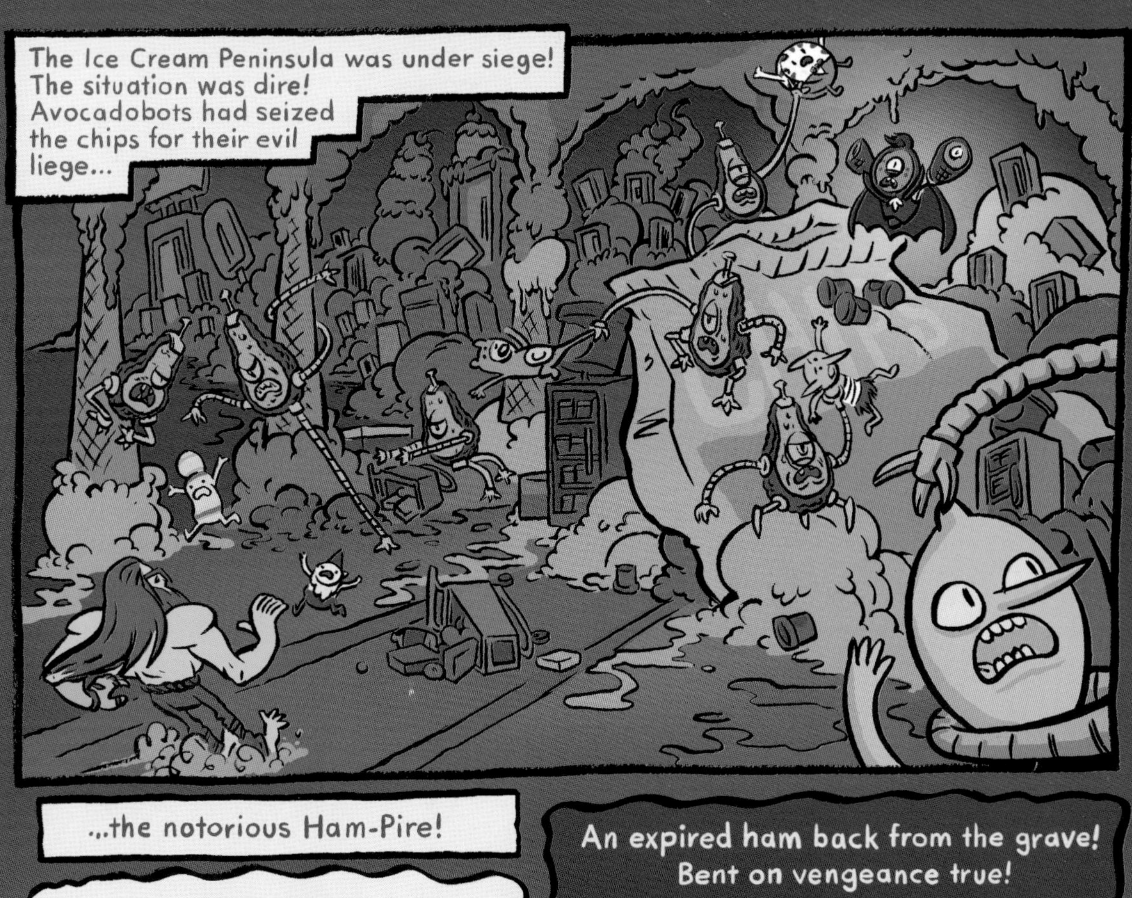
The Ice Cream Peninsula was under siege! The situation was dire! Avocadobots had seized the chips for their evil liege...

...the notorious Ham-Pire!
ALL WILL BE HAM!

An expired ham back from the grave! Bent on vengeance true!

Billy knew that he had to be brave... Or else he would be through!
NOTHUNG!

And so the hero threw down hard!
He made those villains pay!

He smashed and squished
and smacked and sparred...

...those 'bots into guacamole!

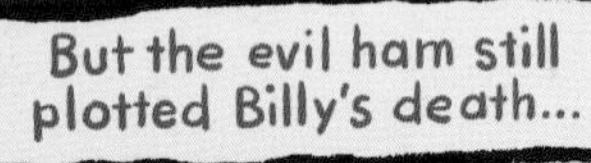
But the evil ham still
plotted Billy's death...

...and Billy could not resist, the deadly power of his ham-clove breath!
And the force of his ham fists!
It looked as though Billy was through, That his legend was at its end!
But in his heart Billy still knew...
He couldn't let down his friends!

The Ham-Pire regrouped his Avocadobots! On Billy they converged!
FLUSH AWAY HUNGER
YAY!
FREE
FREE INSIDE ROBO DOMINATOR
SEIZE CONTROL OF EVIL ROBOTS!
But Billy had a clever plan...
...that turned the tables on their scourge!
The Ham-Pire was felled! Nothing left to do...
...but for Billy to check out!
SALE!
But with the party about to fall through, He'd no time to mess about!

With the Elephant's help, Billy headed back...
YOU BOUGHT THE PEANUTS, RIGHT?
...and returned with the ice cream sublime!
KISSH!
But to his surprise, he found out...
BIRTHDAY JAMZ
Hey! There was more ice cream in the back of the freezer the whole time!
And so Billy learned a universal truth
One that I shall deem.
When you want a party to rock all night...
...you can never have too much ice cream!
...and that's how Billy saved the party!
...boys?
...Hey! Why are you wise guys giving me the high hat?
I'm trying to teach you a valuable lesson about ice cream and perseverance!
THIS IS APPLESAUCE
END!

BEACH BUM BOOGIE

ISSUE TWENTY SIX COVER C
EMILY HU

BEACH BUM BOOGIE
By zack "moonDoggie" giallongo
I DUNNO, DUDE. ALL I'M PICKIN' UP IS SHELLS AND OLD DIAPERS.

C'MON, JAKE-JAKE. THERE'S STILL A WHOLE STRETCH OF BEACH LEFT!
OH, WAIT, DUDE!

I AM *DEFINITELY* PICKIN' UP SOME AWESOME NOSE-SMELLS NOW!

NO DIGGIN'
WHAT IS IT?
OH, MAN! IT'S... *IT'S...*

SKATEBOARDS WITHOUT WHEELS!
NAW, DUDE! THOSE'RE SURFBOARDS!
I KNEW THAT!

SURFBOARDS...
BWOOP!
MOST EXCELLENT SALUTATIONS, MAMMAJAMMAS!
CARE TO PARTAKE IN SOME TUBULAR ANGLING?
WHOA, DUDE!
WAH-HAHAHAHA!
SURFBOARD! WHAT DO I DO?
CATCH THAT BANZAI PIPELINE!
FWOOOSH!
YOU'RE PRIMO!
YEEAAHH!!!
GET READY FOR EL ROLLO, HODAD!
WHHOOAAAAAAAAAARGBL!

I FEEL LIKE SUCH A DWEEEEEEB!
NO WAY, JAKE! YOU'RE TOTALLY, UH, PRIMO!
OH NO! JAKELOOKOUT!
WIPEOOOUUUUT!
AHH! SURFBOARD! WHAT NOW?!
GONNA HAVE TO GET CHOPPIN' AND WALK THE NOSE, BOSS!
BOOT!

WOO HOO! DO IT, MAMMA-JAMMA!
NOW I'M HANGING TEN!
BLITZ THAT CRUNCHER, ACE!

I NEED TO GET BACK UP TO ITS FACE!
NO PROB, BOB! GONNA BE JUST LIKE SHOOTIN' THE PIER!

STAB!

SPLOOSH!

AHOY, GREMLINS!

WHERE'D THAT MONSTER GO? WHO ARE YOU?
MY NAME IS WILSON. I SENT THE MONSTER TO TEST YOU, BUT I'VE SEEN ENOUGH! YOU ARE BOTH PRIMO SURFERS.

THESE ARE MY BROTHERS, CARL AND DENNIS. SINCE YOU'VE PROVEN YOURSELVES, YOU'RE WELCOME TO USE THEM WHENEVER YOUR HEARTS NEED TO BE FILLED WITH RADNESS.

COOL!
DON'T YOU NEED TO USE THEM?
NAH, I'VE NEVER BEEN MUCH FOR SURFING ANY-WAYS. SEEK THE GOOD VIBRATIONS, DUDES!

GNARLATIOUS!
the end!

BOOTY AND THE BEAST

ISSUE TWENTY SIX COVER CB

CRAIG ARNDT

CraigArndt

"Booty and the Beast"
WRITTEN & ILLUSTRATED BY
JEN BENNETT
COLORED BY
EMILY WARREN
LETTERED BY
HANNAH NANCE PARTLOW
CAKE, ARE YOU SURE THE CONCERT'S IN HERE?
YEAH, I'M GETTING CRAZY-EVIL VIBES FROM THIS FOREST.
NOT EVIL! "CREEPY." SAYS SO ON THE FLIER. "NO CARES OR DUTIES, COME FOR WILD SONGS AND BOOTIES!"

GEE, I WONDER WHICH ONE YOU'RE EXCITED ABOUT?
I'VE NEVER MADE SECRET MY APPRECIATION FOR THE SUPERIOR POSTERIOR.

RIGHT, BABY?
::SNORT::

IS THAT MUSIC?
IT SOUNDS ANNOYING.

WHOA.

UGH, POP MUSIC.
MORE LIKE POOP MUSIC, HEHEH... HEH.
UH... GUYS?

THERE'S SOMETHING WEIRD ABOUT THIS CONCERT...
You are my dream...
You're the prettiest thing
I've ever seen...

WHAAAAAAAT?!

I wanna make you my queen~
Red, you make me wanna scream!

WHAAAAAAAT?!

EVIL BOY BAND!
EVIL BOY BAND!
OOOOOOH! COME ON, HONEY! WE GOTTA GET IN ON THIS ACTION!

WHOA!

CAKE!
THOSE SEAT-SHAKING JERKS HAVE GOT EVERYONE UNDER A SPELL!

I'M GOING TO KICK THEIR SEATS!
WAIT, FIONNA! THIS IS SOME SERIOUS MAGIC... BUT MAYBE IF WE...

"NO CARES OR DUTIES, COME FOR WILD SONGS AND BOOTIES!" IF WE SING AND SHAKE OUR GLUTES WE CAN LURE THE ZOMBIFIED FANS AWAY!

AND THEN I'M GONNA PUNCH THEIR GLUTES!

Booties Booties Booties Booties Booties over here!
UH—BOOTIES OVER HERE!
I'll never give you away, keep you with me 'til the end of days
Without you I'd lose my head, because you are my—

IT'S WORKING!

WHOA, RUDE!

MAYBE IT'S THE SONG? WE CAN TRY--
RED!

ALL THOSE "I LOVE YOUs" I WISH I'D SAID
RED LIKE MY HEART, RED LIKE A ROSE—
RED LIKE THE CURTAINS WAITING TO CLOSE—
RED LIKE THIS WOUND THAT KEEPS BLEEDING
DESPITE ALL OF MY DEMON HEALING—
OH HEY, YOU KNOW THE SONG?!
OHHH. UH-OH...
IT'S NOT JUST SONG, IT'S EMOTION! A SONG WITH EMOTION IS THE KEY TO THE SPELL!
THAT'S WHY I'M OKAY! BUTTS ARE NICE BUT FEELINGS MAKE ME SUPER UNCOMFORTABLE!
DO YOU HAVE ANY BUG MILK?
HUH?
YOU TOOK MY RED, STRETCHED IT OUTTA SHAPE UNTIL ALL THAT'S LEFT IN MY HEART WAS HATE!
TELL ME WHYYYYYYY~
TELL ME MOM, WHY'D YOU TAKE MY CHUCKS~
WORE THEM WITH YOUR MOM FEET UNTIL THEY WERE BITTER HUSKS~

YAAAAAAAAA! HI, MARSHALL LEE'S MOM!

Hi, Fionna--

KICK!

OW!

MALOSO VOBISCUM ET CUM SPIRITUM
BYE, MARSHALL LEE'S MOM!

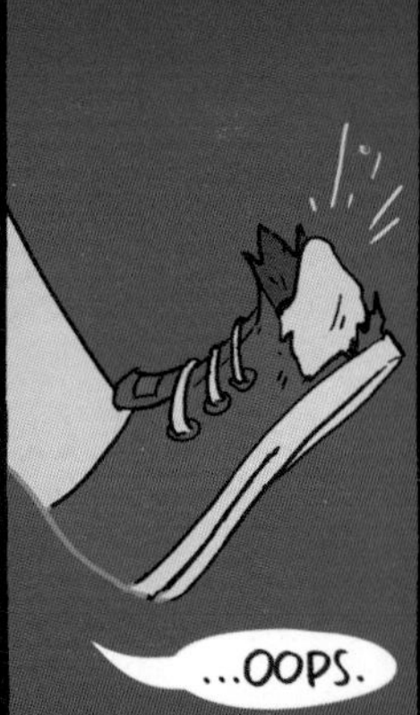

end.

A BUN'S LIFE

ISSUE TWENTY FOUR COVER D
EVA CABRERA

WRITTEN AND ILLUSTRATED BY KRISTEN NESS

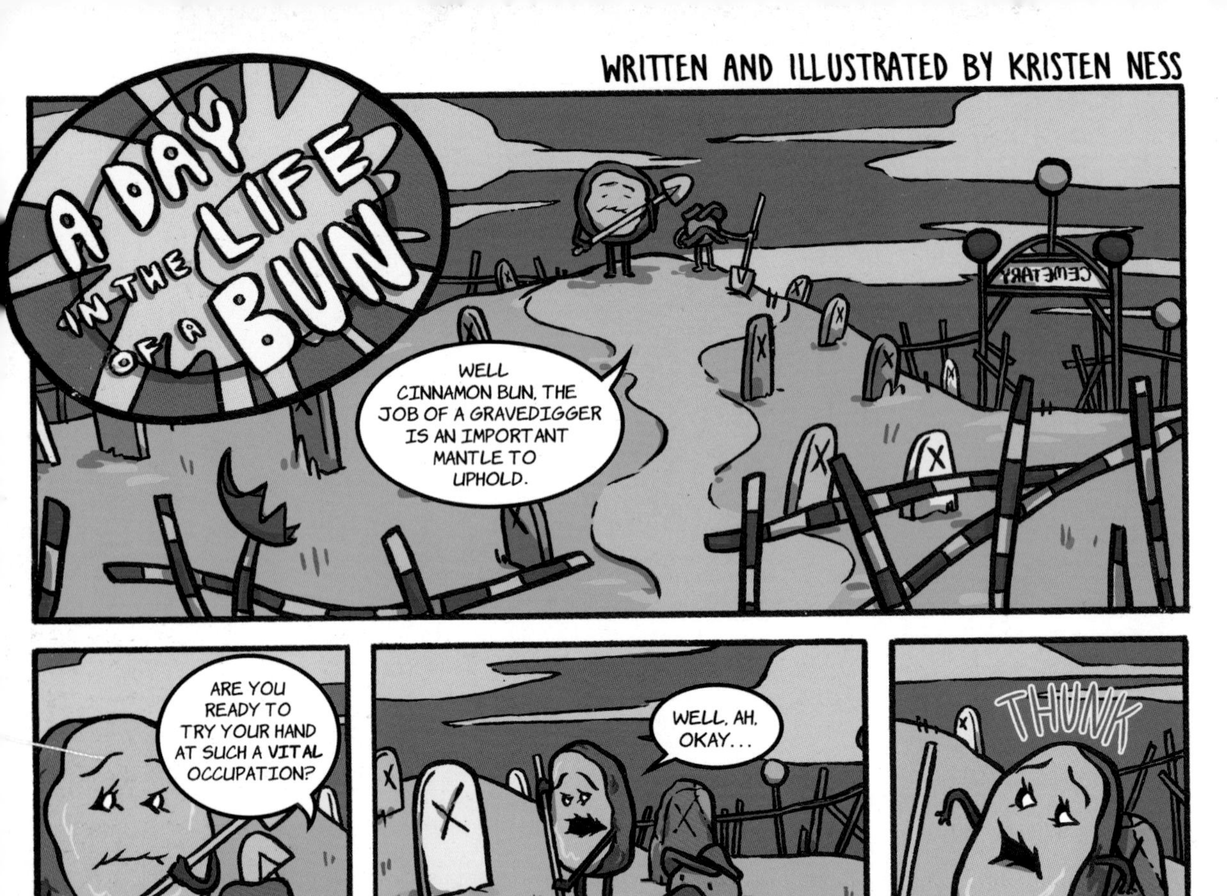

THERE WE GO. NOW YOU'RE READY FOR SOME BUTLER-TRAINING.
NOW THE FIRST LESSON OF BEING A BUTLER IS SERVING. IT'S IMPORTANT TO LEARN HOW TO STACK TABLEWARE.
OBSERVE
HERE I GO...
CRRRAK
I'LL JUST UH... SEE MYSELF OUT.

ALRIGHT, CINNAMON BUN. TRY THIS.
HEY, C.B.!

NOW YOU--

IT'S ALL RIGHT, DR. ICE CREAM! I FEEL FINE! WATCH!

HOP
HOP
HOP
HOP

CLATTA
NEEDLES

I THINK IT'S BEST IF I TREAT HIM . . . ON MY OWN.
I DON'T FEEL SO GOOD . . .
NEEDLE

HMMMMM
I'VE GOT IT!
CINNAMON BUN! THIS IS THE FINAL ADDITION, HAND ME THE SERUM NEXT TO YOU!

SCIENCE MACHINE

GO BACK TO WHATEVER YOU'RE SUPPOSED TO BE DOING!
CRNCH

HISSSSSS MORTAL! ONE DAY I WILL ESCAPE AND LAY WASTE TO THE WORLD ABOVE!
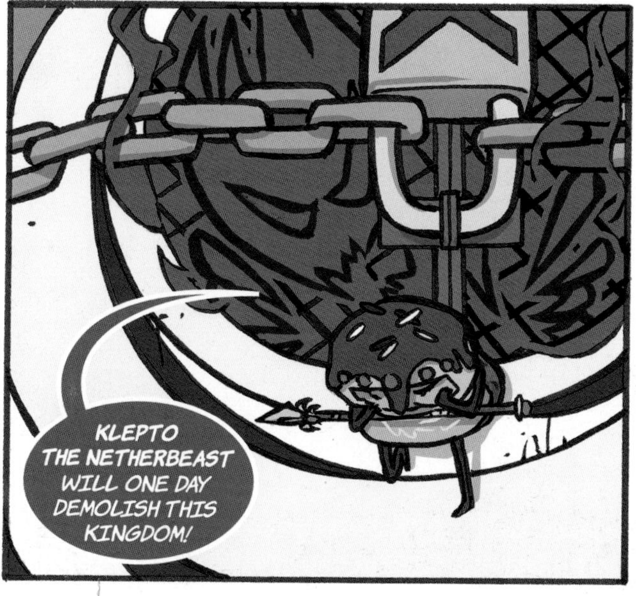
KLEPTO THE NETHERBEAST WILL ONE DAY DEMOLISH THIS KINGDOM!

GUESS IT'S BACK TO THE OLD JOB.
END

SPHAGNUM SHMAGNUM

ISSUE TWENTY FOUR COVER B
BRAD MCGINTY

SPHAGNUM SHMAGNUM

BY JAMES the STANTON

LOOK FINN, JUST THE OTHER DAY YOU WERE SAYING THAT YOU'VE NEVER BEEN OUT ON A BOG BEFORE.

WELL, CHECK THIS OUT!

WOOHOO!
SQUISHY SQUISH

WHOAH!

THIS THING DOES FEEL PRETTY WEIRD!
LIKE I WAS SAYING, THIS IS ONE OF THE WEIRDEST PLACES I KNOW!

?!
RELAX BUDDY!

WE'RE NOT TALKING ABOUT YOU, AND EVEN IF WE WERE-

WE LIKE WEIRD STUFF SO IT WOULD BE A COMPLIMENT!

BE CAREFUL THERE'S A LOT OF GRUMPS LIVIN AROUND HERE, THEY DONT GET A LOT OF SUNLIGHT THIS DEEP IN THE SWAMP.

CONSTANT DARKNESS AND SECLUSION CAN MAKE SOME FOLKS REAL GRUMPY.

AND WATCH OUT FOR SOFT SPOTS OUT THERE!

WHAT THE CATFISH IS GOIN ON UP THERE?!

WHAT ARE YOU DOING!? I TOLD YOU KIDS NO JUMPIN ON MY ROOF-LAWN! GET OFF MY LAWN!

GLENN! YOU DIDN'T TELL ME WE WERE HAVING COMPANY!
GRBLE GARBLE GURBLE
WHY ARE YOU TALKING LIKE THAT?

OH A LAND LOVER ARE YE? HERE USE THE GUEST SNORKEL, IT'LL HELP YOU BREATHE.

SPURT
HERE!

I WAS JUST FIXING SUPPER.
EWH!

I HAVE NO IDEA WHERE MY HUSBAND IS.

DELICIOUS!
MUNCH MUNCH
MUNCH MUNCH
HERE! HAVE HIS PORTION TOO!

THIS IS A PRETTY NICE SPOT YOU'VE GOT FOR YOURSELF BACK HERE.

SORRY MY BUDDY AND I WERE JUMPIN ON YOUR ROOF.
HEY ITS NO BIG DEAL MAN, I'M LESS AGITATED NOW THAT I'VE GOT SOME FOOD IN MY BELLY.

AND BESIDES, IT IS PRETTY FUN TO JUMP ON THIS THING. WHERE IS THAT BUDDY OF YOURS ANYWAY?
THANK YOU!!!!!

YOU WERE RIGHT, JAKE, THIS IS A PRETTY STRANGE CORNER OF THE WORLD AFTER ALL.
COME ON, FINN, LET'S ESCARGO HOME!
END

JELLY WARS

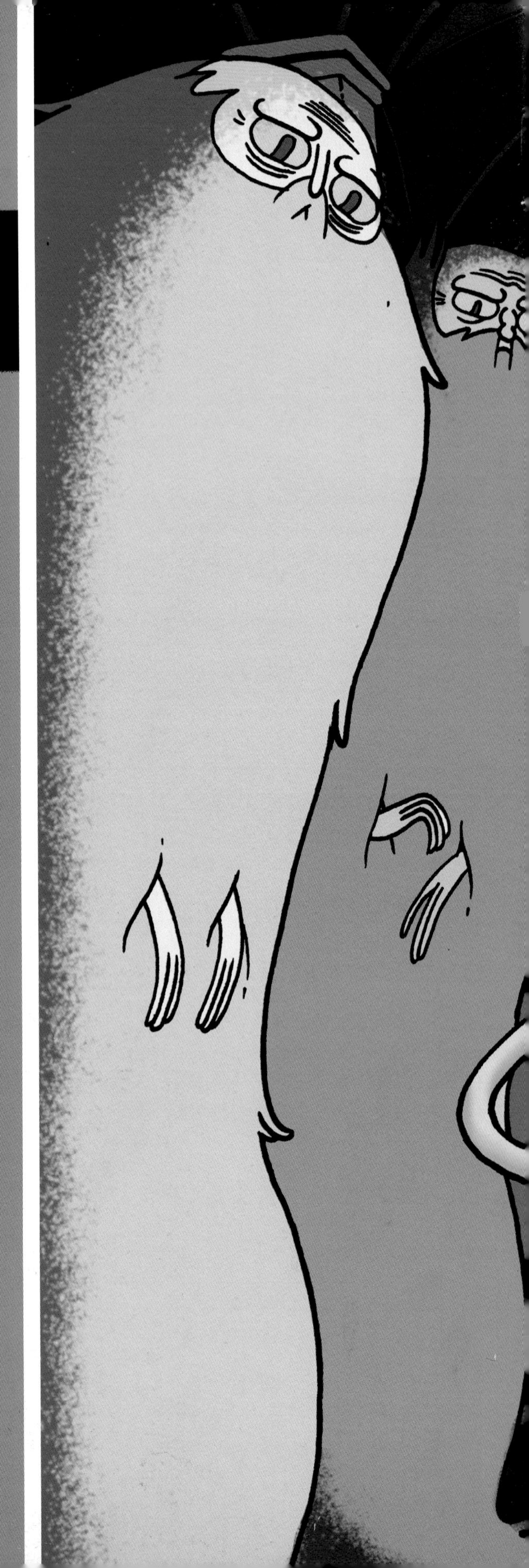

ISSUE TWENTY THREE COVER A

MIKE HOLMES

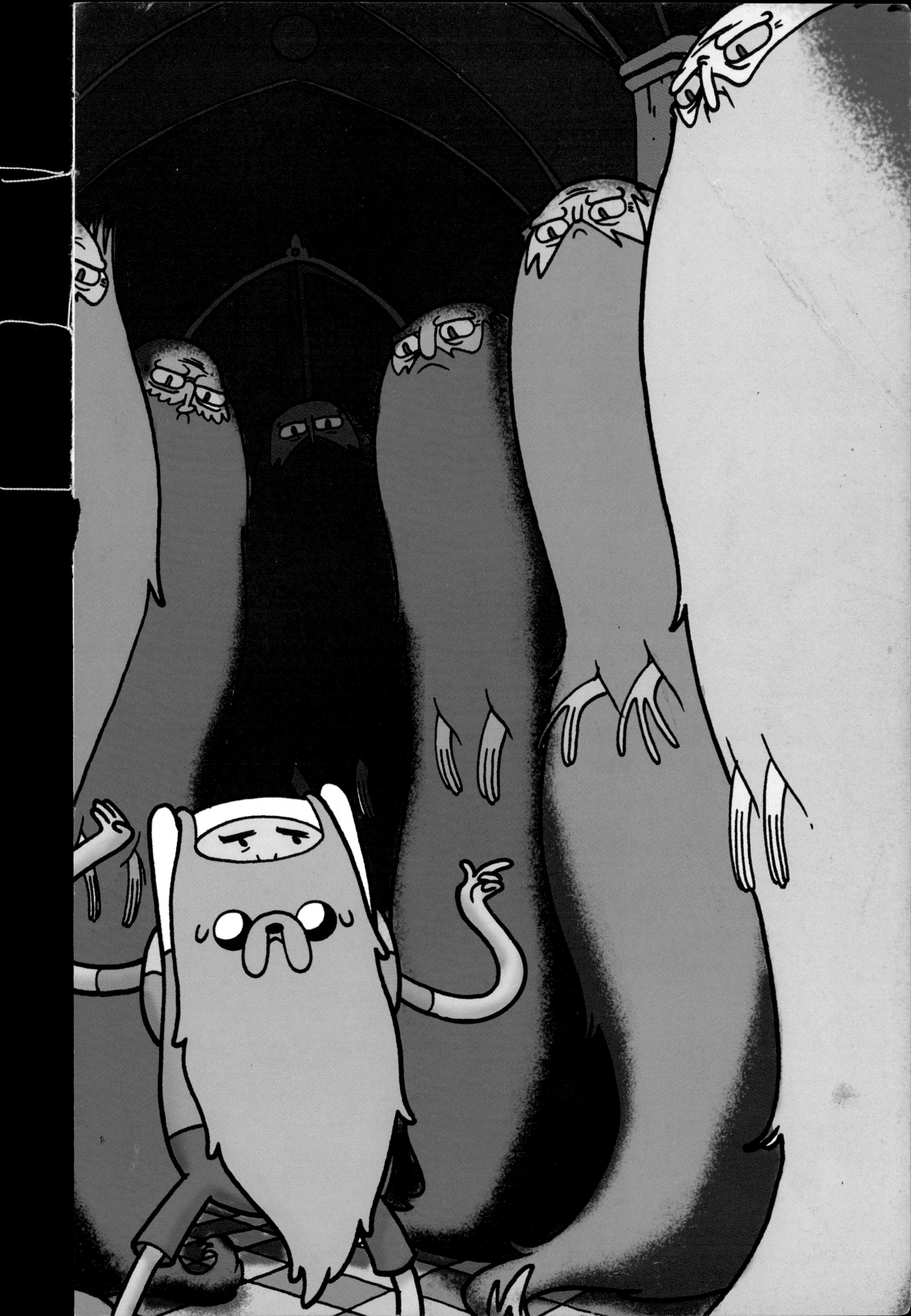

"JELLY WARS"
Written by Eric M. Esquivel
Illustrated by Phil Jacobson
THE LAND OF OOO IS A REALM OF INFINITELY AWESOME POSSIBILITY, MADE UP OF DOZENS OF WEIRD, ENCHANTED DOMINIONS FULL OF WEIRD, ENCHANTED LITTLE PEOPLE.
THIS IS ONE OF THOSE PLACES. IT'S CALLED "THE UNITED JELLY KINGDOM".
IT'S A PEACEFUL LAND, CO-RULED BY THE PROUD PRINCESSES OF TWO NOBLE, JAM-INFUSED DYNASTIES...
MAKE IT RAIN, SISTAH!
YOU GET SPRINKLES! AND YOU GET SPRINKLES! AND YOU-
HECK YEAH!

SO OF COURSE THIS JEALOUS DORK IS GOING TO TRY AN' MESS THINGS UP.
PSST. HEY, GRAPE JELLY FILLED PRINCESS?
YEAH?

STRAWBERRY JELLY FILLED PRINCESS SAID THAT YOU'RE NOT FILLED WITH GRAPE JELLY AT ALL.
SHE WHAT?
WHAT'D SHE SAY I WAS FILLED WITH?

THERE WAS SOME TALK OF DIRTY SHORTS AND STALE FOOD...

THAT'S IT, I HEREBY DECLARE CIVIL WAR!

PST, HEY. STRAWBERRY JELLY FILLED PRINCESS.
YEAH?
GRAPE JELLY FILLED PRINCESS SAID THAT SHE'D RATHER BE FILLED WITH SCORPION EGGS AND KITTY LITTER THAN STRAWBERRY JELLY.
SHE WHAT?

THAT'S IT... I TOTALLY DECLARE CIVIL FREAKING WAR!
WHAT'S SO CIVIL 'BOUT WAR, ANYWAY?

I GOTCHU NOW, FINN!
NO WAY, JOSE!
PEW
PEW
BMO

KERRASH

GASP!
BMO

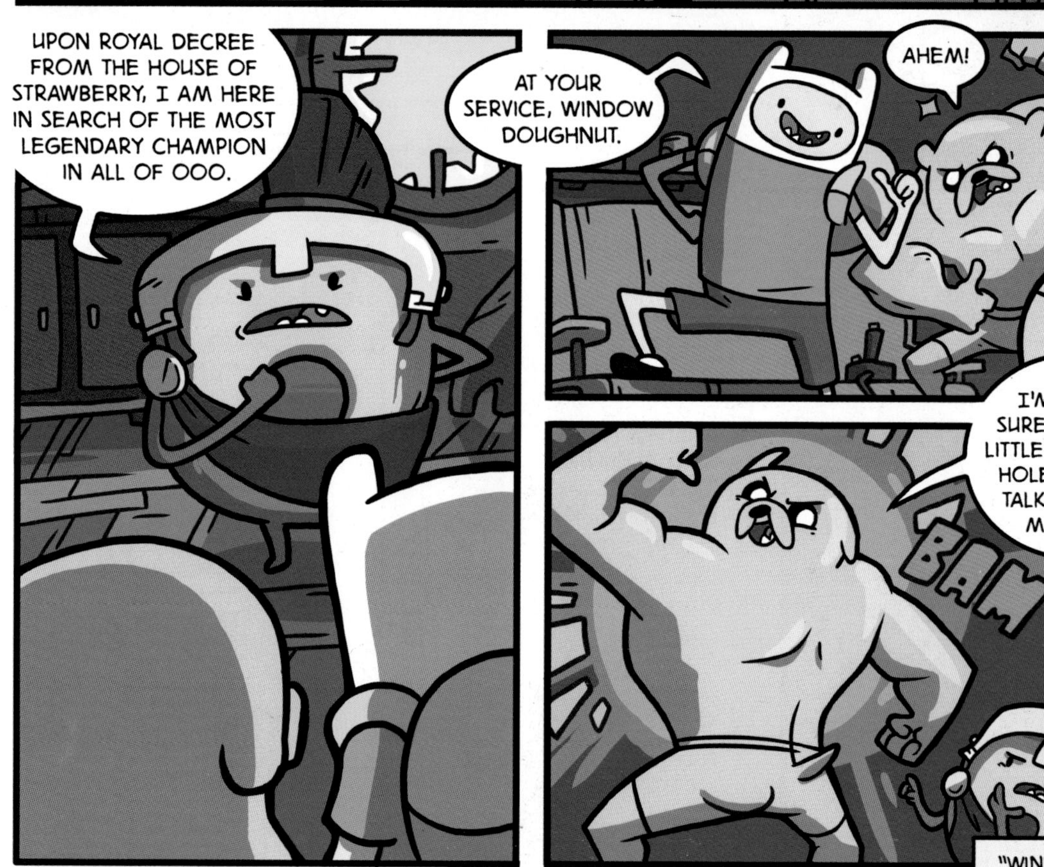

UPON ROYAL DECREE FROM THE HOUSE OF STRAWBERRY, I AM HERE IN SEARCH OF THE MOST LEGENDARY CHAMPION IN ALL OF OOO.
AT YOUR SERVICE, WINDOW DOUGHNUT.
AHEM!
I'M PRETTY SURE OUR NEW LITTLE DOUGHNUT HOLE BUDDY IS TALKIN' ABOUT MOI, BRO.
BAM
YOU ARE "FINN, THE HUMAN"?
"WINDONUT." HEH.

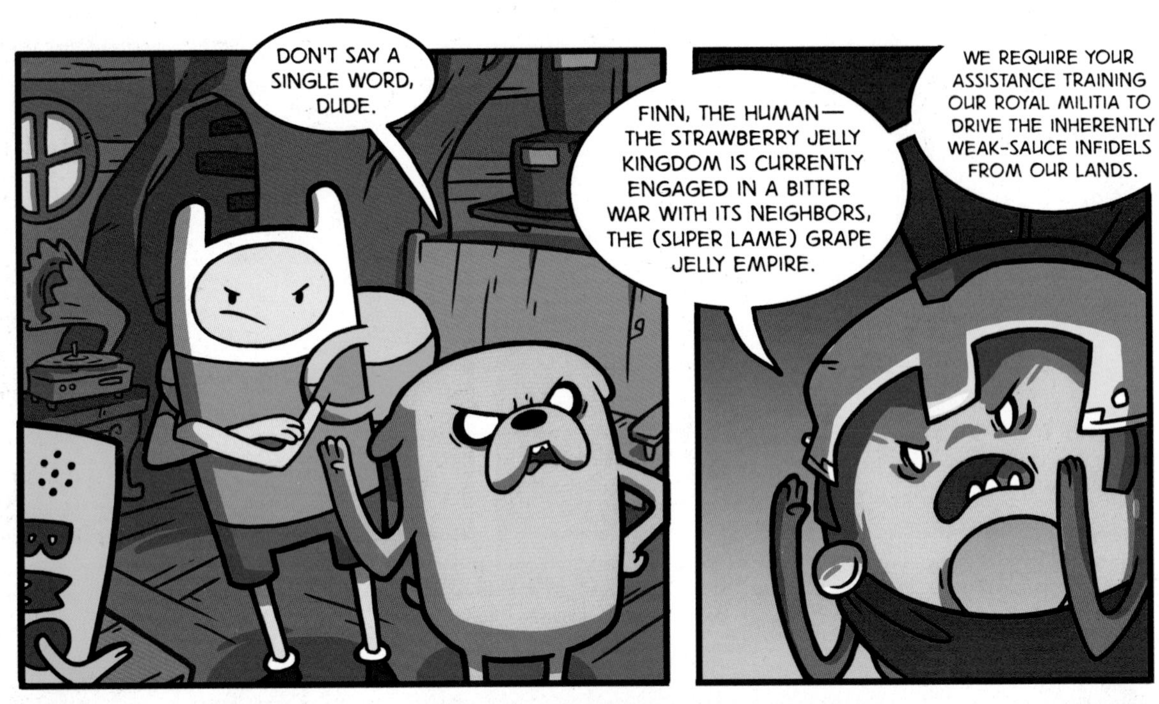
DON'T SAY A SINGLE WORD, DUDE.
FINN, THE HUMAN— THE STRAWBERRY JELLY KINGDOM IS CURRENTLY ENGAGED IN A BITTER WAR WITH ITS NEIGHBORS, THE (SUPER LAME) GRAPE JELLY EMPIRE.
WE REQUIRE YOUR ASSISTANCE TRAINING OUR ROYAL MILITIA TO DRIVE THE INHERENTLY WEAK-SAUCE INFIDELS FROM OUR LANDS.

"INHERENTLY WEAK-SAUCE"? I DON'T LIKE THE SOUND OF THAT...
YEAH, MAN. NOBODY IS BORN WEAK-SAUCE, YOU HAVE TO CHOOSE TO BE. THAT'S WHAT MAKES BEING WEAK-SAUCE SO LAME.
IT'S SIMPLE MATH.

WORD.
COULD BE THESE GRAPE PEOPLE JUST GOT A BUM RAP. LIKE, A MISUNDERSTANDING OR SOMETHING. BROAD GENERALIZATIONS LIKE THAT ARE ALMOST ALWAYS--

I AM AUTHORIZED TO OFFER YOU A REDONKULOUS AMOUNT OF TREASURE, VEGAN TAQUITOS, AND PRINCESS' PHONE NUMBERS IN RETURN FOR YOUR SERVICES.

THOSE WANNABE RAISINS MUST BE STOPPED AT ALL COSTS!
LET'S DO THIS!
UH..
WELL THAT ESCALATED PRETTY QUICKLY.

SO, THE THING ABOUT SLAYING YOUR ENEMIES IS THAT YOU CAN'T BE AFRAID TO GET IN THERE AND REALLY BOOK 'EM A ONE-WAY-TICKET TO OUCH TOWN.
HERE, WATCH!
HIYA
HAYO!
HOO

WHEW. ALRIGHT, NOW YOU GUYS TRY!
RIGHT ON, YOU GUYS!
THAT'S SOME TOP-NOTCH SLAYIN!
FACT: OUCH TOWN'S CHIEF EXPORTS ARE SKINNED KNEES AND HURT FEELINGS. I DON'T EVEN KNOW WHY ANYONE GOES THERE.

YOU GRAPE JELLY FILLED PRINCESS?
THAT'S THE NAME ON MY UNDERWEAR!
LISTEN—I DON'T WANT TO TELL YOU HOW TO LIVE YOUR LIFE, BUT THE STRAWBERRY KINGDOM IS HIRING LEGENDARY CHAMPIONS LIKE IT'S GOIN' OUT OF STYLE.
AND YOU THINK YOU FIT THE BILL, STRETCHY ONE?
MOS DEF, YOUR ROYAL FLY-NESS. YOU'D BE HARD-PRESSED TO FIND ANYONE TOUGHER THAN YOURS TRULY IN ALL OF OOO.
AH. SO YOU ARE THE "FINN, THE HUMAN" CHARACTER I'VE HEARD SO MUCH ABOUT?
UH..
YES.
SERVANTS! FETCH OUR NEW CHAMPION THE CUSTOMARY REDONKULOUS AMOUNT OF VEGAN TAQUITOS.
DON'T FORGET THE TREASURE, YOUR MAJESTY.
AND THE TREASURE!
...AND THERE WAS TALK OF PRINCESS' PHONE NUMBERS?
AND THE PRINCESS' DIGITS!
YOU'RE LUCKY YOU'RE NOT WEARING PANTS, JAKE, 'CAUSE THEY'D BE ON A WHOLE BUNCH OF FIRE RIGHT NOW. YOU BIG LIAR, LIAR.

FOR THE GLORY OF THE GRAPE EMPIRE!
FOR THE VEGAN TAQUITOS!
FOR THE PRINCESS' DIGITS!
FOR THE HONOR OF THE HOUSE OF STRAWBERRY!
RARGH!
GRR!
AHA! TAKE THAT!
SLICE
FROM HECK'S HEART, I STAB AT THEE!
WAIT, LOOK!
CHECK IT OUT, YO!
WHY...YOU'RE NOT FILLED WITH PUNGENT PURPLE...
AND YOU'RE NOT A STARCHY CONTAINER OF SEEDS...
IS THAT CUSTARD?!
WE'RE NOT SO DIFFERENT AFTER ALL!
JUDGING PEOPLE IS STUPID.
SO IS WAR. LET'S KNOCK IT OFF FOREVER.
IT'S BEAUTIFUL, MAN.
YEAH.
THIS WAS YOUR PLAN ALL ALONG, WASN'T IT?
YEP. SURE WAS.
MINE TOO.
THERE'S NO WAY THAT WAS THEIR PLAN ALL ALONG, YOU GUYS.
THE END

ISSUE TWENTY SEVEN COVER B

SABRINA SCOTT

ISSUE TWENTY SIX COVER A

GENEVIEVE FT

BMO

DISCOVER
EXPLOSIVE NEW WORLDS

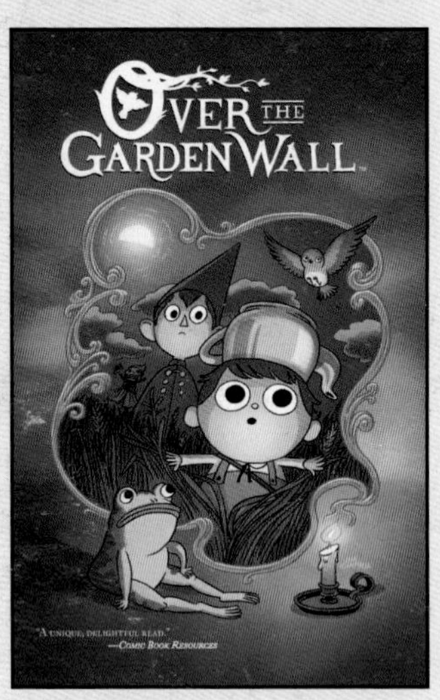

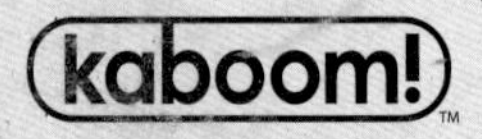

AVAILABLE AT YOUR LOCAL COMICS SHOP AND BOOKSTORE

To find a comics shop in your area, call 1-888-266-4226

WWW.**BOOM-STUDIOS**.COM

Adventure Time
Pendleton Ward and Others
Volume 1
ISBN: 978-1-60886-280-1 | $9.99
Volume 2
ISBN: 978-1-60886-323-5 | $14.99 US
Adventure Time: Islands
ISBN: 978-1-60886-972-5 | $9.99

Regular Show
J.G. Quintel and Others
Volume 1
ISBN: 978-1-60886-362-4 | $14.99
Volume 2
ISBN: 978-1-60886-426-3 | $14.99

Regular Show: Hydration
ISBN: 978-1-60886-339-6 | $12.99

The Amazing World of Gumball
Ben Bocquelet and Others
Volume 1
ISBN: 978-1-60886-488-1 | $14.99
Volume 2
ISBN: 978-1-60886-793-6 | $14.99

Over the Garden Wall
Patrick McHale, Jim Campbell and Others
Volume 1
ISBN: 978-1-60886-940-4 | $14.99
Volume 2
ISBN: 978-1-68415-006-9 | $14.99

Steven Universe
Rebecca Sugar and Others
Volume 1
ISBN: 978-1-60886-706-6 | $14.99
Volume 2
ISBN: 978-1-60886-796-7 | $14.99

Steven Universe & The Crystal Gems
ISBN: 978-1-60886-921-3 | $14.99

Steven Universe: Too Cool for School
ISBN: 978-1-60886-771-4 | $14.99

Peanuts
Charles Schultz and Others
Volume 1
ISBN: 978-1-60886-260-3 | $13.99

Garfield
Jim Davis and Others
Volume 1
ISBN: 978-1-60886-287-0 | $13.99